"Why do I want to bad so...badly?"

It was freeing, this sensation. Louisa threw her head back and laughed.

"We can be a little bad," he murmured as he lowered his head, his lips skimming her throat. Her laughter stopped on a gasp, the sensation of it like an electric shock. His lips gentle, drifting over her skin. There was no laughter now. The only sound from her was half sigh, half moan. Her nipples prickling in her bra. Heat arrowing between her thighs. The need for him, all-encompassing.

She wanted. Like she'd never wanted anything or anyone before. It overwhelmed her, her whole body a mess of sensation.

Did he want her as much as she craved him?

His lips traced back toward her face, her jaw. Light brushes till she turned her head and their lips touched. Breaths intermingled. Slow, luxurious. Hypnotic. She became a captive of the sensation. Opening for him. His tongue slipped into her mouth, the barest of touches with her own.

Then the kiss slowed, stopped.

Matteo pulled back, looked deep into her eyes. Pupils blown wide, his own irises almost black.

When **Kali Anthony** read her first romance novel at fourteen, she realized a few truths: there can never be too many happy endings, and one day she would write them herself. After marrying her own tall, dark and handsome hero in a perfect friends-to-lovers romance, Kali took the plunge and penned her first story. Writing has been a love affair ever since. If she isn't battling her cat for access to the keyboard, you can find Kali playing dress-up in vintage clothes, gardening or bushwhacking with her husband and three children in the rain forests of South East Queensland.

Books by Kali Anthony

Harlequin Presents

Revelations of His Runaway Bride
Bound as His Business-Deal Bride
Off-Limits to the Crown Prince
Snowbound in His Billion-Dollar Bed

Behind the Palace Doors...

The Marriage That Made Her Queen
Engaged to London's Wildest Billionaire
Crowned for Her Royal Secret

Visit the Author Profile page
at Harlequin.com for more titles.

Awoken by Revenge

KALI ANTHONY

HARLEQUIN
PRESENTS

HARLEQUIN®
PRESENTS™

Recycling programs
for this product may
not exist in your area.

ISBN-13: 978-1-335-59355-9

Awoken by Revenge

Copyright © 2024 by Kali Anthony

Harlequin Enterprises ULC
22 Adelaide St. West, 41st Floor
Toronto, Ontario M5H 4E3, Canada
www.Harlequin.com

Printed in Lithuania

MIX
Paper | Supporting
responsible forestry
FSC® C021394

Awoken by Revenge

As a wise woman once said to me...even the smallest flicker of light can overcome the darkness.

CHAPTER ONE

AN AMPHIBIAN WAS giving her trouble. Louisa pushed her glasses up her nose, staring down at the recalcitrant creature she'd sketched. Her illustration brief had been clear. He was meant to be a cute frog with a golden crown. The perfect frog prince for a sweet children's story. Instead, he sat there on the page, crown jauntily askew. His froggy little mouth turned up into a kind of smirk. Arms crossed, as if in some way judging her…

Louisa could never accept that. No judgement was allowed anywhere in her life, any more.

Though it was a familiar smirk on that mouth of his. Sly, knowing. Recognition niggled in the recesses of her memory, yet she still couldn't place it. Louisa blew out a slow breath. Sometimes your characters worked against you and today was that day. She tried sketching him again, this time with a billowing cape. A rakish wink.

Although surely frogs in children's stories shouldn't be rakish, should they?

'Play nicely,' she said to the frog on the page. She could have torn the paper out, tossed him away and shown him who was the real boss, yet something about his familiar smile forced her to keep him for now. Louisa turned to a fresh sheet of crisp white paper. She would get him right. She *would*. She had a deadline for her illustrations, and she never missed a deadline. Timing was everything. She lived by it.

Instead of challenging herself with misbehaving frog princes, she immersed herself in the world of the story. A verdant, magical forest, with fairies and animals come to life on the page. A mythical world where she didn't have to think about a gleaming coffin lowered into sodden ground in a snowdrop-carpeted cemetery. A grave in the English countryside her great-aunt Mae had loved and would lie in for ever.

Louisa rubbed at the yawning ache in her chest. No. She didn't have to think of grief. Right now, she could think about another world entirely. A world of make-believe. Her favourite place.

She inked a watercolour wash of green, the detail of leaves. It was as if she were in that picture, strolling through the forest like a lost princess with the breeze whispering through her hair. Possibility abounding as her brush slicked across the page and her heart tripped along at the mystery of *discovery*. Half in reality, half out of it. Picking up some blue because in this world she created the sun always shone and the sky remained a perfect hue…

A clanging gong sounded in the distance. She tried ignoring it, even though the doorbell could challenge Big Ben for loudness. A ringing doorbell couldn't be right. It was Wednesday, and no one was due today. The house empty, staff on one of their days off. Just her and her work, in what should be blissful silence. Of course, tourists would occasionally drop by on days the home wasn't open to the public, but a polite sign on the door usually saw them on their way. Anyhow, since Mae's passing Easton Hall had been closed, which was made clear on the house's website. No. Everyone in the area knew the home's schedule, and none would be impolite enough to disturb it. She could ignore the demanding sound with impunity…

Yet the knowledge that there must be a stranger outside gnawed at her consciousness like a worm in an apple. Louisa stilled. Her brush held above the page, a splat of blue dripping onto it as she was rudely wrenched from the world of her illustration into cold, hard reality.

She looked down at the livid blue blot now bleeding over the page, marring her picture. At least it was only a working drawing, and not the final copy. The error wouldn't put her behind her schedule. Louisa loathed the idea of missing her deadline almost as much as she loathed unscheduled strangers at the door. In recent times those kinds of strangers hadn't meant anything good.

That infernal doorbell gave another chime. Whoever it was wasn't going away. Since Mae had been laid in the ground, a number of people had visited the property. Buyers' agents, mostly. Looking to see if Easton Hall was for sale, given the owner's passing. All vultures, as if the estate were some kind of carcass to pick away at, rather than a loving home.

She could try to ignore them, yet they were known for their doggedness and the housekeeper, Mrs Fancutt, and her two Pomeranians weren't here to help her evict them. Right now, she was alone.

It was her job to see the intruders off the property.

'There's more to the world than you've experienced, Louisa. Be brave.'

The last words Mae had spoken to her. Tears pricked Louisa's eyes, but she blinked away the burn. Her great-aunt had lived a long and eccentric life and had loved Louisa fiercely. Swooping in when one medical professional had *finally* refused to believe her mother's lies. Giving her a home when her mother had died just prior to a trial that would have laid ugly secrets bare.

That Louisa wasn't sick all those years as her mother had claimed.

Mae had ensured she'd gone to school again, trying to give her a normal life. Getting her the help she'd needed when her mental scars had threatened to overwhelm her. If Mae's last message to her was to be brave, that was what she'd be. In her twenty-four years, she'd fought bigger demons than strangers on her doorstep.

Louisa washed her brush. Pulled her long hair back into a rough ponytail and stomped to the front door. Realising as she peered through the spyhole to an amorphous blur that she'd forgotten to take off her reading glasses again. But what did it matter? She'd be working again in no time and sometimes the world was better when everything was a little soft focus. She took a deep breath, turned the giant iron key, and yanked the ancient oak door open.

A man in dark clothes stood on the gravel drive with his back to her, seeming to survey the land before him as if he owned it. Whilst he was at an inconvenient distance for her glasses, his silhouette could only be described as *sharp*. His hair like a blot of ink on his head. Something about him made the heat creep up her chest and prickle her cheeks.

Everything about his demeanour screamed authority.

She wanted to say something, but she feared her voice was trapped and all that would come out was a croak. Then he turned. Began to move towards her as if he were made of liquid, his movements so rolling and fluid. The only thing making her realise he had solidity and weight was the heavy crunch, crunch, crunch of his shoes on the gravel drive. And she had to say something because he'd get to the stairs soon and she had a wild premonition that if he made it to the top, he'd never leave...

She held up her hand. 'Stop right there.'

He did. Closer now, a little less soft focus. The corner of his mouth quirking in a way that seemed all too familiar. That sensation of recognition overcame her. Give him a billowing cape, a jaunty crown and a rakish wink and this man was her frog prince made human.

It was as if she'd drawn him to life.

Her heart thumped an uncomfortable rhythm. She should take off her glasses, but she didn't want him to think that she wanted to get a better look at him, even though she did.

Desperately.

'You haven't answered any of my lawyer's correspondence.'

That voice of his. Smooth, rich and decadent. Like treacle tart with clotted cream. *So good*, yet *so bad* if you indulged too much. Louisa was sure this man could make reading chess moves sound like some kind of midnight intimacy... But correspondence? That sounded official and *not* like an estate agent. All things official she left in the hands of her solicitor. Any mail redirected there. Although the man had talked of retiring and sometimes did seem increasingly overwhelmed in his small, over-stuffed office in the village.

Though…this man spoke almost as if he knew her. How could that be? In recent years whilst caring for Mae she'd not ventured much further than the local village and if he'd lived there, she would have remembered him. He wasn't the sort of person you'd ever forget. Sure, every-one in the local area knew her. In the early days of her arrival, she'd been *'Poor Louisa Cameron…' 'Lost her parents…' 'Too young to be living with an old lady…'* She'd heard it all. Once, those whispers had chattered in her head. Especially when she'd believed that someone would come to take her away from the only home she'd felt safe in for years.

'Everything goes to my solicitor. He must be busy.'

Even though the man was soft focus at the bottom of the stairs, she saw his brows rise on his high forehead. 'What you call busy, I'd call incompetent. You weren't at the reading of the will.'

Mae had told Louisa she'd be looked after. *'You will always have a home.'* Her solicitor had confirmed that Easton Hall was her place to live, for ever. Why would she need to go to the reading of a will with all her rela-tives? If she never saw another Bainbridge again, it would be a happy day. They didn't deal with life when it became real and messy. Elegantly brushing said messiness under vast antique Axminster carpets so it wouldn't tarnish the family's pristine name.

All they cared about was their money, their reputation and keeping up appearances. The ones who had come to visit Mae nearer the end had tried to ingratiate them-selves. Get her to leave here for a care facility, *'for her*

own good'. But it was never about what was good for
Mae. Only themselves. Each of them wanted a piece of
the Bainbridge estate, Mae being holder of the most coveted prize, Easton Hall and its surrounds. She'd cackle
when they left. *'Watch the silver as they walk out the
door!'* How sad that she hadn't been far wrong. Mrs Fancutt had reported finding one of them poking about the
teaspoons in the good cutlery service after one visit…

'There was no need for me to go. I know everything
I need to.'

'Do you?'

In those final days of Mae's life, she'd promised Louisa she didn't have to worry. So Louisa believed her because Mae had always kept her promises. Of course, if
this man had been at the reading of the will, that meant
he might be a lawyer too. In his dark suit, he had an official kind of demeanour. Except…there was something
more. Standing near the bottom of the stairs with his
hands thrust into his trouser pockets in a casual yet au-
thoritative way, it was as if he were *entitled*.

Bainbridges were the most entitled of the lot with
their wealth, and good name paid for through cynical
attempts at philanthropy to gain kudos, not putting their
money where it mattered most. Yet he didn't look like
anyone from that family with his dark hair and warm
brown skin. Bainbridges tended to an almost vampiric
type of pale. She supposed she was of Bainbridge stock
too, though she didn't look much like the rest of them
with her colouring, taking after her father. Something
she'd come to be thankful for, even though her lumines-
cent mother had bemoaned her red hair, green eyes, and
freckles if she spent too much time in the sun.

'We need to talk, Louisa.'

That decadent voice of his drew her out of her intro-spection. Which was a good thing because introspec-tion was a bad place for her to be even on her best days. He'd begun moving again, slowly this time. One step. Pause. Two steps. Pause. Though she couldn't describe any of the moves as hesitant. Each pause more like a silent demand for permission to move further, from a man she doubted sought permission from anybody, to do anything.

'What are you doing?'

'I thought it was self-evident. Coming closer, since I'd rather have a discussion where I don't have to raise my voice or, even better, need to communicate with two paper cups and string.'

Paper cups and string… What an odd thing to say. Yet a memory came drifting back of a magical summer as a six-year-old, staying with Mae here as she often had when her dad was sick. A common occurrence as the motor neurone disease began to take its awful toll. She remembered exploring Easton Hall. Running wild through the rambling gardens chasing butterflies.

There was a boy who'd come to stay too. He'd seemed so much older and wiser, at twelve. A cousin, Mae had told her when they'd first met. Though her mother had later said he wasn't a *real* Bainbridge because he'd been adopted, as if that were some kind of disqualification. And they'd played, trying to make a string telephone, which had worked in the end, to their surprise.

'I've had so many adventures,' Mae had told them. *'Make your own and make them stupendous.'*

It had been the last moment of happiness before a

whole mountain of misery for Louisa. But she'd created special memories during that time. More importantly, stories of those stupendous adventures had been what she'd recounted to Mae in her last months. Those adventures had made Mae laugh. Maybe Louisa had taken some creative licence, but so much of her past was a blur of sadness and sickness and pain, what did it matter that she exaggerated? Trying to hold on to those few snatches of brightness as tightly as she could.

It seemed as though the sun had always shone in that summer of innocence and joy. There wasn't a day that hadn't been perfect.

The man was halfway up the stairs now, and somehow the squirming sensation in her belly didn't feel like the beginnings of dread, but something far more…anticipatory. Almost like excitement. Though it was remiss he hadn't told her who he was, when he clearly knew her name. As he climbed with his long, powerful legs he became clearer and sharper. As if she were inking in the details of an illustration she'd been commissioned to complete. His suit in a dark charcoal grey, pristine white shirt gleaming in the sunshine like the snowdrops in that old churchyard. As he came closer the niggle of recognition didn't pass. It grew and grew.

Then he arrived at the top of the stairs and that recognition hit her with a wallop. Because that tanned-skinned, dark-haired little boy who she'd thought completely unlike his insipid Bainbridge namesakes, with all his vibrancy and life, was standing right in front of her. All grown up, filled out and angular with broad shoulders, narrow hips and cut cheekbones. His brown eyes she'd once thought of as warm and hinting at constant mischief as a child, now remote and cool. Like the flat stones they'd gathered in the stream running through the estate to skip in quieter waters. He'd taught her how to do that and she'd squealed when her stone had skipped twice.

He'd been less impressed. His had skipped six times. Sometimes more.

He *regarded* her then, seeming to glower in the same ominous way as the slate-coloured sky behind him. A storm threatening. Louisa's breath hitched. She smoothed her hands down the front of her crushed dress. Feeling too soft and unkempt for him as he stood there sharp as a blade. Not a dark hair on his head out of place. The neat stubble on his strong jaw clearly by design, rather than a neglect to shave.

She'd bet he neglected nothing.

'Matty.'

Not his given name of Matteo. He'd been Matty to her. The adopted Bainbridge who'd apparently conquered the world and made his fortune independent of his family. Almost to spite a name that tended to open every door. Yet what on earth was he doing here? He'd not visited Mae in that last year of her illness, or at all in the time Louisa had lived at Easton Hall. Though her great-aunt would mention him and his successes. She had tended to keep some things close, to be tossed out occasionally like little treats of sweets…

'Louisa.'

The way he said her name was soft and smooth, almost like a caress. Though he'd called her Lulu when they were children. Her father's nickname for her. One her mother had loathed because it apparently sounded undignified.

She'd never understood why a child's name needed to be dignified.

'H-how are your parents?'

Louisa wasn't sure why she sounded so breathless, as if she'd run a mile. It was a normal kind of question, wasn't it? Although she had no real practice at small talk, since her contact with strangers was restricted to telling tourists about the history of Easton Hall and its surrounds, which was a well-practised script.

His mouth thinned. Eyes narrowed. That look could slice you clean through, leaving you eviscerated. Then he shrugged, but it was somehow stiff. Almost an attempt to be dismissive when she suspected there was an enmity running seams deep.

'I've no idea. I haven't seen them in years.'

Mae had mentioned some family estrangement, so she didn't press. Especially not to ask about his sister, not right at this moment. She'd gathered even as a child that Felicity was a tender point for him. She'd been envious of the idea of a sibling back then, when she was a lonely only child. Matty had said, almost like a challenge, that he had a sister and she was sick. Louisa had known all about sick people, so she'd left well alone. Even then, she'd wanted the fantasy of a perfect summer rather than being haunted by the spectre of illness and death.

She suspected they both had.

Matty didn't ask about her family in return, but she didn't think that rude. The last time she'd glimpsed him was through streams of tears at her father's funeral, eighteen months after that summer at Mae's. He'd stood there, almost fourteen, sombre in a dark suit looking so grown up to her almost-eight-year-old self. She hadn't cared about anything that day because her world had ended.

'What are you doing here?'

It wasn't as if this were a social visit. All economy and business, he didn't even offer her condolences when she'd spent over half her life with Mae. She wasn't sure she liked it, missing the smiling sunshiny boy she'd glimpsed all those years ago. But then, she'd changed a great deal too. She wondered what he thought of her.

Whether he thought of her at all.

'Had your solicitor passed on any of my solicitor's letters, you would have known.'

His mouth was a thin, stern line. He looked as if he rarely smiled, no laugh lines round his eyes. The consummate businessman he'd reportedly become.

In response, she pasted on her brightest smile, because she'd come to believe life was too short and tenuous not to try and fill it with a little happiness.

'Well, now you're here you can tell me. Would you like to come in for a cup of tea?'

'I could just as well be inviting you inside, Louisa.'

How…odd. His voice was so cold. What had happened to him to strip him of any warmth? She was caught by the inappropriate desire to reach out, to touch. To see if he felt as cold as he looked. The prickle of something entirely unpleasant began to march down her spine. A warning.

'What do you mean?'

His mouth quirked into the pretence of a smile. His lips curling at the edges in a way that should seem happy, yet it didn't touch his eyes. They remained cold and hard as those river stones in the stream running through the estate.

'Since I'm now owner of Easton Hall.'

CHAPTER TWO

'WHAT? NO!'

Matteo didn't tell lies. His life was founded on truth since he knew the pain of lies by omission. No sugar coating. His word was his bond.

He was known for two things in both his personal life and in business. His ruthlessness and his honesty.

He looked at the woman now gripping the old oak door as if it were the only thing holding her up. Her fingers slender and pale, biting into the dark wood. She stood there in a long, soft white dress as if she'd stepped from another time. Like a woman from a pre-Raphaelite era painting, an artist's muse burst from the canvas. With red hair in a thick ponytail over her shoulder. Tendrils loose and curling round her heart-shaped face. Her pale skin dotted with faint freckles he remembered as darker from running in the sunshine over a long-ago summer.

But she wasn't a child any longer. On any objective assessment, she'd grown into an exquisite woman. The heat of admiration curled a seductive journey deep inside.

A woman he should not be suffering errant attraction to. One he was about to evict…

Not evict. Politely ask to leave, with handsome compensation for doing so. And once she was gone, this would represent his sweetest victory. The adopted and disdained Bainbridge inheriting the jewel in the family crown. Its most coveted possession, Easton Hall. A dream he'd had since his nineteenth birthday when he'd finally cut the false cord that had tied him to this family that wasn't his by blood. The family that had all but abandoned their adopted child in favour of their natural-born one.

He knew those who considered themselves the 'true' Bainbridges wouldn't like it, and he was prepared for the fight. They were crooked to the core, if his quiet investigations into their charity interests were anything to go by, and had far more to lose than he did. In fact, they were unable to match him in any way. Still, there'd already been murmurings at the reading of the will. Unhappiness that he'd been appointed executor when he wasn't a real Bainbridge, and others claimed to be more qualified. Wanting a part of the vast property riches here when they weren't entitled to any of it. Threats of challenging the will.

They could all go to hell.

He'd vowed then that if there was any way he could take this place for his own, he'd ensure none of that cursed family ever graced its halls again. The house would be lost to them *for ever.*

His victory was almost complete, but for the woman standing in front of him, mouth gaping like a hooked fish.

'Are you going to let me in?' he asked.

They needed to discuss the predicament in which they found themselves. The estate was crumbling. Mae had talked of her worries about it and keeping up with the specialist work this home required to bring it back to its former glory. Especially being asset rich and cash poor, as were so many of those whose money and history were as old as the dirt upon which their homes stood. Mae had refused his help when alive. After her death he'd tried to send out a structural engineer to assess the state of the property, but the man hadn't even been able to set foot in the house. Reportedly being chased away by a terrifying woman and a threat, which seemed fanciful.

'Easton Hall is my *home*.'

She tore off her glasses and looked up at him with her beautiful green eyes. He'd been struck by them even as a twelve-year-old. Reminding him of the freshest new growth of spring. Of the moss at the edge of the stream that ran through the property.

So many of his memories of her had been frozen in that time, of someone small and pretty. A young if sometimes annoying little friend for a child starved of friendship and family, relegated to boarding school. Other boys' families occasionally took him in for school holidays, feeling sorry for him because he had a sick sister. What none of them realised, and what he'd concluded over those long years of her treatment, was that his family had wished he'd been the one to fall ill. The adopted one, instead of the beloved natural child...

The only glimmer of joy had been staying with Mae here, in this old ramshackle house. In that hazy summer where there were few rules, and two children were allowed to run wild in an imaginary world fighting dragons, catching frogs. It was as if the two of them had finally become the children they hadn't previously been allowed to be, when surrounded by grown-up problems like illness and death.

But there was no point to those reminiscences. He hadn't got to where he was, well past his first billion with an impressive property portfolio of boutique hotels and retreats for those who wanted intimacy, luxury and privacy, by having any form of sentiment. Business was the language he spoke, and he was unparalleled in his sphere.

That was his world.

'I'm sure this must come as a shock. I'm sorry for your loss.'

He tried to sound conciliatory, because he needed to work with her. And in some ways, he did feel some sympathy. She'd lived with Mae since before her teens. Being Mae's carer for the past twelve months meant she'd likely have expected to inherit the whole estate herself…

'She needs to be looked after, Matteo. Promise me you will.'

Mae's request during their last conversation. A promise he'd made with no thought, because it had sounded important to her and who was he to deny an old woman some sense of peace? Only now he realised the impact what he'd agreed to might have on his ultimate plan for this place.

Louisa narrowed her gaze. 'It's your loss too. Yet *you* weren't at the funeral.'

Matteo stared right back, ignoring her disapprobation. He wasn't a coward. Though his mobile phone weighed heavy in his trouser pocket. The unanswered messages from his sister, Felicity, saying she wanted to talk, taunted him. He ignored the sensation. He'd been occupied with a deal for a new property in Bali, that was all. She knew he was busy.

'I was in South East Asia on business. Once I found out, I couldn't make it back in time.'

Mae would have understood. She always did. Wrote him letters, which his assistant opened and scanned, sending them to him via email. A card each birthday… He and Mae would talk on the phone, about Easton Hall, about taking care of her interests. Talked a little about Louisa and her talents as a children's book illustrator too. How Louisa had come to be like the daughter Mae had never had. Then their last call, which he'd realised only after her death had been her goodbye to him. One full of warmth, where she'd told him how proud she was of him. And she'd made him make the promise he was now beginning to regret.

'She needs to be looked after.'

Still Mae had left its execution to his own judgement. He could do more to carry out her wishes, here, now, than he could ever have done when she was alive, given she was so stubborn and headstrong. As much as it had frustrated him, he'd admired her for that. Taking on Easton Hall after her husband had died, almost unheard of when the natural course would have been for Great-Uncle Gerald to have left the home to his nearest male Bainbridge relative, rather than his young wife…

Now, Matteo studied the young woman standing inside the home that he would soon add to his property portfolio. A woman who looked soft and innocent, and in need of the protection he'd promised. All he knew of the world was that it was cold, hard, and unforgiving. How would Louisa navigate that now Mae was gone?

'Felicity came,' Louisa said.

Those words tore him from his introspection. Felicity hadn't ever met Mae. Why had she even been at the funeral?

'I'm glad she could make it.' He tried to sound charitable. The words ground out of him, as if forced.

Louisa cocked her head, inspecting him in some way. For what, he wasn't sure, though it gave him a sort of prickling feeling at the back of his neck, almost as if she was judging him.

'She seems well.'

Everyone in the family knew of the tragedy of Flick, as they all called her. The child whose birth had been seen as a kind of miracle, till she'd become cursed by a childhood leukaemia diagnosis. Then her remission and apparent cure seemed like another miracle.

'I understand she is.'

'She's your sister. Don't you know?'

He could sense the judgement that infused every word. Louisa didn't have siblings, so how could she possibly understand? He and his sister didn't talk about it, when they talked. Her past forgotten. She'd reached out to him about five years earlier on his birthday and that was how it had been between them since. Texting. Calling on the celebrations. Birthdays, Easter, Christmas. That had always been enough.

'We both travel for work. There's not much time to talk.' Louisa seemed to be good at picking at his old wounds. Time to shut the conversation down. 'Unlike now. I have all day to speak with you and keeping me out here isn't going to help. There are things we need to discuss.'

Louisa hesitated for a moment, worrying on her pink bottom lip with her teeth. 'I was told I'd have a home for ever.'

He might have cared once, when he'd been capable of it. But that child with the capacity to love and care was gone. Ground out of him by constant disappointment. Love didn't matter. Caring didn't matter. People shouldn't be disposable, yet he'd learned that he was. Twice. His birth mother, whoever she was, abandoning him on a hospital doorstep. Then the family who'd adopted him, who hadn't wanted him either. Not when they finally had a child of their own blood…

Blood always won out, in this family at least.

They hadn't cared about him, until he'd become successful. *Finally* claiming him as a Bainbridge when he craved to rub their noses in the certainty that he wanted nothing to do with them. Would have changed his name to eschew the family completely, had he known who he really was. But all his searches had been fruitless. Not even genealogy DNA testing, his last hope of finding his birth family, had turned up a relative. It had only given hints at his heritage. Italian. Which accounted for his colouring and his name. It gave him nothing more.

He was truly alone.

'You'll be looked after,' Matteo said. He'd promised Mae, and he delivered on his promises. Louisa would see reason. He'd ensure that she was well compensated, with a bank account so fat and full she could do whatever she dreamed. Travel the world, buy a home of her own, drape herself in jewels. He'd learned over the years that was what people wanted.

His riches.

She might look innocent and guileless, but she'd be no different.

No one he'd met ever was.

Louisa could barely catch her breath, as the heavy weight of dread crushed her chest. She hardly believed a word Matty said. He had to be wrong.

Yet why would he lie?

No, it would be okay. It *had* to be okay.

Still, a voice inside Louisa's head shouted a warning that if she let him in, she'd lose the only home she'd ever really had. The only place she felt safe. She was torn between being polite and listening to that voice.

The same voice that had whispered once that she wasn't really sick. That it was her mother making her ill, hurting her whilst claiming it was love. The voice that had told her she needed to get *someone* to listen because no doctor, no matter how clever they were with all their medicines and needles and procedures, could make her well.

That voice had saved her life.

But this was *Matty*.

She looked up at him, towering above her. Broad. Strong.

Handsome…

No. Why was she thinking like this? He'd come to take away…everything. Then he raised an eyebrow, his lip quirked. And in a flash, he wasn't Matty at all. He was the man that boy had grown into. Matteo Bainbridge. Carrying an arrogance and assertion that seemed to hold her in some kind of thrall. An almost cool disdain for everything around him. Something about it made her tingle all over, though she didn't like to think too hard why that was.

Mae had always taught her to be polite. To be a good hostess, even though her great-aunt had stopped entertaining years ago. But one thing Louisa was certain of: had Matteo arrived on Mae's doorstep whilst she was alive, she would have welcomed him in with open arms.

Louisa felt obliged to do the same.

She forced herself to prise her fingers away from their death grip on the door. Stand back a little, although she wanted to slam the ancient wood firmly in his face because that door had protected the home from any number of invaders in the past.

Still, if he really did own the home, she needed to hear what he had to say.

'Okay, come in.'

None of that sounded like a good hostess, at all. Still, Matteo's lips curled into a smile that looked every bit the frog prince she'd just drawn, and kind of gloating as well.

'Thank you.'

She gestured him inside as he seemed to sweep in exactly as if he owned the place. Which, if she believed him, he did. He cast an appraising eye over the threadbare Axminster, looking around him as if searching for what was wrong, rather than focussing on what was right.

'Follow me to the kitchen.'

He didn't follow, of course he didn't. A man who looked as if he ruled the world wouldn't follow anyone. He moved into lockstep beside her, but it seemed almost uncomfortable. As though he had to adjust his pace, slow it to fit hers.

'Where's Mrs Fancutt?' he asked. 'I'd like to speak with her about chasing away my structural engineer.'

Louisa missed a step, falling behind Matteo's long, powerful stride. Hurried to catch up. She didn't want Mrs Fancutt getting into trouble. She was Easton Hall's long-term housekeeper. If Matteo was telling the truth and the home was really his, the woman deserved to be kept on in the role.

'She did no such thing.'

She rather had, with a little help from Louisa, but Matteo didn't need to know that.

'Comments about setting the dogs on him and talk of muskets sound familiar?'

Maybe it did but she'd never admit it. The heat rose to Louisa's cheeks. She hoped he wouldn't notice.

'Mrs Fancutt owns two Pomeranians who aren't in the least bit threatening…' At least that was the truth, though the man who'd arrived claiming to need to inspect the house didn't know that. 'And it was an invitation to see the armoury, where there might be a tiny bit of damp around a window frame. Your structural engineer seems to lack any kind of fortitude. Heaven help him if he came across a decent bit of dry rot. He'd be overcome.'

'You seem to know a great deal about the conversation.' Matteo's voice was smooth and cool as silk.

If he blamed her, then so be it. 'Why wouldn't I? I have a vested interest in avoiding trespassers on the property.'

'He wasn't a trespasser, he had my permission.'

'Well, he didn't have mine.'

'What are you going to do? Set the unthreatening Pomeranians onto me?'

'Sadly, Mrs Fancutt is on a day off. I'm sure she'll be

sorry to have missed you. I'll say hello to her for you. Give Binky and Bess a pat.'

Yet after today, would she have a place here at all? She breathed through a wave of grief that overtook her. The yawning ache that simply opened inside. She'd lost her father, and it had been as if the world had broken apart. Staying in pieces for years. Now she'd lost Mae and, in many ways, it was the same, the corresponding loss of all that was safe and secure. Her world tilting on its axis yet again because those she loved always left her...

'Perhaps I should be making you the tea?' he asked.

That jolted her from her inertia. He was trying to take over already. Take the home that had been hers for twelve years. Louisa straightened her spine.

'I'm fine.' She'd just needed a moment. That was all. She kept walking but, out of the corner of her eye, thought she could see Matteo glancing her way. As if waiting for her to crumble. That wouldn't happen. She might bend, but she wouldn't break.

The kitchens sat quiet and empty given it was a day off for the staff here. She loved the space with its exposed brickwork, worn stone floor and huge stove. She'd thought the room magical when she'd first arrived in the home, food always available whenever she was hungry, because her mother had never fed her enough.

There are things you're allergic to which make you ill.'

Louisa had come to learn, after those years of pain and deprivation, that she was allergic to nothing. It was yet another lie her mother had told in the pretence of love. Making sure to keep her thin and weak, so that she'd appear as sick as her mother claimed her to be.

Louisa didn't know why all these memories were assailing her now. She'd put her past behind her, begun making a future. She didn't want to think about her childhood and that hunger, deprivation and pain. Instead, she placed her glasses on the counter and put on the electric kettle to boil. Made the tea in her favourite yellow teapot, poured two cups. All the while a sensation prickled between her shoulder blades. She tried to ignore it but knew Matteo was watching.

'You said we needed to talk?' she asked, carrying the tea to the table before sitting down. He took a cup, black. No sugar. Looking at her as though she were a bug under glass, and he were conducting an inspection.

An uncomfortable sensation.

Matteo lifted the tea and took a sip, the sunny yellow cup dwarfed in his hands.

'I'm surprised you know so little about Mae's will.'

It sounded like the bite of criticism. Her mother had been an expert in its delivery. She ignored the sting. That didn't mean it didn't hurt.

'When I came to live with Mae, she promised I'd have a home for life. After she died, my solicitor confirmed that I never had to leave Easton Hall. It might be a surprise to you, but I trusted Mae and believed her.'

Matteo looked round the kitchen as if taking stock, his golden-brown eyes cataloguing something he already owned. What did he see? The heart of the home as she did, or that everything was a little worn? The stove in need of restoration. A tap, drip-drip-dripping into the sink.

Then he fixed that assessing gaze on her.

'Apart from inheriting Easton Hall and its contents,

I've been appointed executor of Mae's estate. After some money left to charity, you've inherited the remainder. Her personal effects. Jewellery.'

'What about a place to live?'

His perfect lips thinned a fraction. A tiny muscle in his stubble-covered jaw clenched. Matteo placed his hands on the table, clasped them together. The cuffs of his shirt a gleaming white against his golden skin.

'That's what we need to discuss. Mae's will grants you a right to reside in Easton Hall for as long as you want, until it stops being your principal place of residence…'

A bright spike of relief skewered her. She shut her eyes against the tears that once again threatened. She could stay here. She didn't have to leave. Louisa hadn't known how tightly she'd held herself. How little she'd breathed since she first saw Matty on the doorstep. Her shoulders dropped as she let out a slow exhale. It was as though she began to wilt as some of the tension bled from her.

'…or until you marry.'

Louisa snorted. Marry? Mae had always lived in hope for her and there were things that intrigued Louisa about a marriage. The physical side of a relationship, especially after she'd found those old leather-bound books in a remote part of the library here. An erotic collection of inked prints she'd once pored over. There'd been one of a woman clearly wearing a wedding dress in one of them…

A heat began to ignite in her chest, thread through her veins as Matteo brought the teacup to his perfect lips once more. Took a swig, his Adam's apple bobbing as he swallowed.

'What's so funny about the idea of you marrying?' he asked.

Getting married meant finding a man when she barely went to the village any longer. Where would she even meet anyone? And falling in love? A shudder ran through her.

She'd had first-hand experience of what was done in the name of love. The pain it wrought. Why would she ever look for that?

'I'll leave marriage to other people. Like you, since you sound so keen on it.'

Now Matteo snorted, then checked himself. 'I travel too much to be tied down. Whereas you're young. It might not sound like an attractive prospect now, but it will be.'

As if he were so ancient. 'You're only six years older than me.'

'I left home in my teens and built my business from nothing to be one of the premier luxury hotel groups in the world, whereas you're…'

'What?'

He cocked his head, gaze drifting over her. Likely taking in the dress she wore, in fine white cotton with pretty pintucking and lace. One of her favourites from the number that she'd first found as a teenager in a trunk in the attic, which she'd been told were from one of the previous Bainbridge wives from the early nineteen hundreds. Her clothes were a particular hit when she took tours of the home talking about the history of the place. People thought she dressed up for the role. They didn't realise this was what she liked to wear. And she'd never really cared that it made her stand out, before today…

'You're a young woman who's devoted her life to caring for an elderly one.'

He said that as if it were a bad thing.

'Do you understand love, Matteo?'

He reared back, sitting straighter in the chair. Eyes a little wider. Looking uncomfortable.

'We're talking about property. What's love got to do with this?'

Most of what had happened to her had been kept hidden. The public had never found out about the charges against her mother, just the way the exalted Bainbridge family had wanted, because heaven forbid their perfect name be tarnished. Then her mother died of a heart attack before the press had got wind of what she'd subjected Louisa to. There was no point rehashing the truth when the lie that the last of her parents to pass away was beloved was so much more palatable.

'Mae took me in when I was an orphan.' Had given Louisa a home when all she'd had to look forward to was foster care, because no other Bainbridge had had any interest in her and her problems. Her father had been an only child with no relatives left to care for her. 'Everyone else in this family was only ever interested in the family name, or what Mae might have been able to gift them. Mae gave me far more than material things. She gave me a home, a safe place to land. And I loved her for it. Why wouldn't I care for Mae?'

The woman had sacrificed years of her later life, looking after Louisa, more a mother than her own ever had been. Had made sure she'd received the professional help she'd needed to overcome the death of her father and her mother's abuse. Louisa would have done *anything* to repay her.

'I'm sure there are many things you'd like to do now

that your caring duties are over. I have a proposition for you.'

She'd had a lifetime as a child being told what was good for her, especially by men like the various doctors who'd 'treated' her, believing her beautiful, fragile-appearing mother when she'd said there was something terribly wrong with her only child.

For years, no one had believed Louisa. She'd become tired of her voice not being heard. It remained a struggle to speak up some days, because she was still unsure anyone listened.

'Of course you do.' Her voice came out too soft, too quiet. Louisa was simply pleased she could get the words out at all.

'I want Easton Hall outright, and I'm prepared to pay well for you to relinquish your right to reside here.'

She stilled. Her heart almost missed a beat. If she agreed to that…

'Where would I live, then?'

'Anywhere else you want.'

A tight band wound round her chest. Crushing the air from her. She could hardly breathe again. This home was the only place in the world she'd ever felt secure. All she had. Mae had promised she'd always be safe, and Louisa had believed her when there was no one else in the world *to* believe. There was nowhere else to go. She *couldn't* leave here.

'You haven't been listening. This is my *home*.'

'It's an old house, which is in dire need of restoration. Mae neglected it. Given that, I have an offer for you.'

He smiled, and *this* time it met his eyes. That smile was glorious. Some might call it a winning smile. Matteo reached into the inner pocket of his suit jacket. Pulled out a folded white piece of paper, placed it on the tabletop and slid it over to her. She opened it. It was an official-looking document that talked about giving up her rights under Mae's will for a sum of money. She stilled.

All those zeros at the end couldn't be right. She'd never seen so much in her life. The offer was designed to be an amount no one could refuse…if money was what you were interested in.

'Why do you want Easton Hall so badly? It looks like you're offering me an extraordinary deal. Surely that's bad business?'

Matteo's eyes narrowed. 'What does it matter to you if you're going to take it?'

And there was the part where she knew he could never understand, what this place meant to her.

'It matters to me. You're probably a man who has homes all over the world. Why this one?'

He shrugged. Sat back in his chair. Head cocked. Eyes cool and assessing as if weighing her up again.

'The home will be well utilised. My company, Arcadia, will turn it into a boutique retreat.'

So, not a home. She looked about the old kitchen that had fed generations of families. Thought of Mrs Fancutt, who'd been here most of her working life, managing the house, doing the cooking. Of all the people who worked to keep the house going. Generations of families had been employed here. If it became a 'boutique retreat'…

'Will the staff be "well utilised"?'

'Given that they're all older, they'll be comfortably retired, which I'm sure they'll enjoy.'

'Have you asked them?'

'I beg your pardon?'

'Have you asked whether they'd enjoy it? Do you know the answer to that question?'

All the times they'd sat here in the kitchen at this old table in the evenings, Mae included, and played cribbage or other card games. Betting with toothpicks as if they were made of gold. He'd never understand this wasn't just a job to them. At the funeral, there'd been punishing grief. These people had been promised jobs, and homes for life too. On the day Mae had passed, each of them had said they wouldn't leave here, leave Louisa. It was more than her home; it was theirs as well.

She shook her head. 'No, this isn't happening.'

'What do you mean, *"This isn't happening"*?'

Louisa folded up the piece of paper, which held no temptation for her at all. Slid it back across the table-top to him.

'Thank you for your kind offer, but I'm not leaving.'

The change in him was profound. His eyes narrowed, the colour of them turning. How warm brown could suddenly look ice cold she wasn't sure, but he achieved it. She'd kidded herself even thinking he was the boy she'd met so long ago. The memories of that time entertaining Mae in her last months—they were a mere fantasy. This man before her had no sentiment. He was all calculation.

'I'll add another hundred thousand.'

The way he said it. Who could toss money around like that with no care?

She shook her head. 'If Mae knew what you were planning, she'd turn over in her grave.'

Matteo stood, planted his hands flat on the tabletop.

'She knew *exactly* who I was. Ask yourself, why

didn't she leave the home to you? A woman who spent what should be the best years of her life caring for an elderly lady. Surely you'd have expected repayment for that? It must come as a terrible shock that you weren't made executor too. That the house was left to me. But Mae assessed my experience and my resources, and she clearly made a judgement about yours. She knew that looking after this place was beyond you, which is why I'm here. I'm doing you a favour.'

Each word shot like another poisoned arrow deep into her heart. Tainting memories of a woman Louisa had thought she'd known. Yet he didn't understand. Matteo would take this place and tear the soul out of it. Tear apart everything she loved. She couldn't let him.

She smoothed her trembling hands over her dress. Stood. She'd made a terrible mistake allowing him to come in here. Underestimating him. She wouldn't again.

'Thank you for your considered offer, but I've heard enough. You can leave now.'

'That's where you're mistaken, Louisa.'

The way he said her name, as if he was in some way mocking her. She gritted her teeth. 'How am I in any way mistaken?'

'Thinking that I'm going to leave. I own the house, and I'm moving in.' He crossed his arms. Mouth a thin, cold line. The ominous grumble of thunder rolled in the distance. 'Today.'

CHAPTER THREE

MATTEO WOKE TO a ferocious wind howling outside, as rain lashed the rattling windows. Even though Easton Hall was made of stone, it was as if the whole house trembled against the storm's onslaught.

He'd taken the spare room he'd used here as a boy that single summer he'd stayed. Ignoring Louisa's mutinous glares as he'd brought his bags inside and removalists had come with a small truck to drop off computer equipment. If she refused to move out, then she'd have to get used to him moving in. Living here meant nothing. He had no house in the UK. On the odd occasion he was in the country, he stayed in one of his hotels. This was as good a base as any and the home needed to be assessed. He could use the time to do that, and to convince her to leave in the process.

He had all the time in the world to spare for *that* project.

Matteo tried closing his eyes, but his mind ticked over with work. Sleep had been an elusive state in his life. Owning an international business meant it was always daytime, somewhere. Right now, he had too many ideas crowding inside his head of how to turn this property into the newest jewel in his hotel chain's crown. Giving his clientele the type of authentic 'English country house' experience they'd pay handsomely for.

With those thoughts whirring through his head, he gave up all pretence that he'd get to sleep any time soon, and turned on the bedside lamp, which lit the room with a dim glow, occasionally flickering as the flashes of lightning and cracks of thunder raged outside. Grabbing his mobile phone from the bedside table, he made a note to ask the engineer he'd rebooked to assess the building's lighting protection system, assuming it had one.

Matteo propped his arm behind his head, and scanned his emails, seeing a report from his chief operating officer about a prospective property in Spain. Through the window ahead of him, flickering blue lights reflected in the glass slicked with rain. He ignored it, but a piercing cry rent the darkness. He sat bolt upright. What was that? A vixen's cry? Though how could it be? It was the wrong time of the year and most definitely the wrong weather for that.

Matteo strained to listen for the noise again over the wind and rain. In the end, he left the comfort of his bed to investigate, dressed only in his boxer briefs. He raked his hands through his hair and peered outside at the persistent flashing lights close by. An emergency vehicle, he assumed as gusts of wind hurled at the home in a vicious assault. A tree down across the road? An accident? Who could tell? Anything was possible in this weather.

As he watched, a blazing white light burst outside with an instantaneous crack and boom. The lights in the room died. Matteo gripped the window ledge, heart thrashing in his chest. He enjoyed storms, the power of nature, but that had to be a direct strike on the house. Apart from the roar of the wind it was as if an ominous silence fell over Easton Hall, before he heard a creak and groan as if the home itself moaned in protest. All of him stilled. Waiting. For what he didn't know, a sixth sense filling him with dread.

He turned on his phone torch and went to the door of his room, opened it. Above the noise of the storm there was a faint crackling sound. A taint to the air, like burning plastic. Smoke?

Fire.

Louisa.

He didn't think as he strode down the hall. The torch app from his phone cast its trembling light in the darkness. He coughed at the thickening acrid scent. Electrical? No flames. In the ceiling?

They had to get out.

'Louisa!'

Matteo knew from a multitude of fire-safety plans for his hotels that these old buildings were a tinderbox of ancient wood, ready to ignite. If on fire, in no time the whole place could explode over their heads.

'Louisa!'

The chill air bit his naked skin. Threadbare carpet felt rough under his feet. He tried to remember her door. Which one? Guess. He pounded on the dark oak outside one room. Would she be asleep? Somewhere else in the house?

Movement made him stop. A figure in ghostly white appeared as the door in front of him partially opened. Hand up against the light of the phone torch he'd pointed her way.

'Matty, what happened?'

She coughed. The air thicker, hazy.

'Lightning. We need to leave now.'

She froze. Gripping the door as if paralysed.

'C'mon. We have to go,' he snapped through gritted teeth as she stared at him with her huge green eyes, wide in what looked like terror. Yet she still didn't move.

'Take my hand, Louisa.' He held out his arm. Hand, palm up. As the wind still rattled the home round them, he willed his breathing to stay calm, measured, as she reached out, paused, drew back.

'I—I haven't… M-my things. My art. I can't.'

Then an alarm burst to life, another and another with their shrill and piercing sound. She clapped both of her hands over her ears.

Enough.

'We don't have a choice.'

This was taking too long. He stepped forward and simply swung her into his arms. She didn't fight. There was no struggle. Louisa went limp as he held her tight. His phone in one hand attempting to light the way as he tried to keep as low as possible, the air a flare of grey, thin smoke in front of him as they both coughed. Finding the stairs. A crash sounded. Falling masonry? Louisa flinched in his arms. He gripped her tighter, her body soft against his.

'We'll be okay.'

It was a promise. When he made those, he kept them, since so often in his life promises made to him hadn't been met. By some miracle he found the stairs, began walking down as fast as he could, reaching the bottom and heading through the house towards the front door as voices called out.

'We're okay,' he shouted. As he did, a beam of light cut across them.

'No one injured?'

He shook his head as firefighters and police milled about in the entry, escorting them towards the front door.

'Anyone missing?' a firefighter asked. Droplets of water on his uniform glittering in torchlight.

'Not us.' Matteo drew Louisa closer to him, 'There are some staff who live here. It's their day off. I don't know if they got out.'

'They all seem accounted for, sir. You might check, after we get you seen by the paramedic.'

Matteo nodded as they walked through the front door into a carnival of flashing lights of emergency services. The frigid gale hit him like a slap. He'd forgotten he was only partially dressed, the weight and heat of Louisa against him keeping him warm. Somehow tethering him, not letting the fear of what might have been get too much of a grip on his consciousness.

Around them, emergency services worked. Kept him moving forwards. The gravel of the drive was sharp and cutting on his bare feet. Someone wrapped a blanket round him. Led him to an ambulance. He told them their names. Relinquished Louisa even though he didn't want to lose the sensation of her in his arms. The perfect fit. Sat as the adrenaline that had been rocketing through his body bled away and the world simply spun round them.

Against the backdrop of night, flames licked the roof of the house. Then hoses. Water jets. Shouts and movement. The warm glow of fire guttering. Dying. Igniting again in a fight to remain alive.

Little by little he came back to himself. Turned round as Louisa was huddled on a gurney.

If he hadn't been awake. If the fire alarms hadn't worked. If emergency services hadn't been close...

If he hadn't been here at all and Louisa had been alone in the house.

No.

Louisa coughed. Eyes wide as the ambulance officers asked questions. Not answering them.

'We've inhaled some smoke.'

They came at him with an oxygen mask but he waved it away. 'I'm fine. Look after her. I think it may be shock.'

The ambulance officers nodded, placing a blanket round Louisa too, covering her soft, sheer nightgown. It struck him then how out of place she was in all of this. How breakable she appeared.

Something of himself seemed to break inside too. At how fragile life could be. How one day everything seemed fine and the next, everything changed. One moment he'd had a healthy little sister, then came the unexpected bruising. The listlessness. Till her awful diagnosis. The chemo. The infections. Constant terror that one day he might come home and she'd be gone, for ever.

He stood. No. He'd hardened himself to it all and the pain of that time had gone away. He didn't need to remember. Tonight, there were things he had to do. Plans to make. He'd wanted to get Louisa out of the house, and the universe had granted him the perfect opportunity.

'I have staff to check on,' he said to the ambulance officers. 'Can I go?'

Louisa seemed to wake up from her inertia. Sat bolt upright on the gurney.

'No!'

'They need to check you over,' Matteo said.

She shook her head violently, her hair swirling round her shoulders. 'I'm fine.' Tried to get up. Swayed. Her breaths short and shallow.

She looked just like Felicity had. Dark rings under her eyes, stark in the harsh light. Skin so pale she was almost translucent. Memories came flooding back of Flick being taken away in an ambulance all those years ago. The old fears. He shut them down.

'Let them look at you.' He made his voice stern. The voice of the businessman whose staff did exactly what he asked when he asked it. Louisa's eyes widened, mouth trembling. He wished then that his tone had been gentle. But he had no time for softness and gentleness. That had ended in his teens. And yet he couldn't move. Heart still pounding behind his ribs as if fighting for an escape.

'Don't let them do anything to me.' Her voice was the barest whisper.

What in hell's name would they do to put that fear on her face?

'It hurts, Matty.'

One of the last conversations he'd had with his sister as a child, when she'd been in hospital, undergoing the awful treatment that would save her life. It was as if a hand grabbed his throat and began throttling him.

Had something like that happened to Louisa? No, it couldn't have. She'd been a healthy child the last time he'd seen her at her father's funeral, and Mae had told him nothing. Though whatever the reason, he knew fear when he saw it.

'I'm right here. I won't go anywhere.'

Matteo wanted to do more. Overcome by the almost overwhelming desire to take her into his arms again. Smooth his hands over her. Tell her it would all be okay. Hold her. Yet that made no sense. Shock, that was it. Like her, it must be affecting him too. The desire to cling to the nearest life. Instead, he pinned the ambulance officers with a glare of warning.

'They won't *do* anything to you other than check you over. Isn't that correct?'

One of them nodded, turned to Louisa. 'We'd like to take your blood pressure. Listen to your heart and lungs. Is that okay?'

Louisa looked at him, almost pleading.

'I'll hold your hand if you're afraid,' he said.

'Okay,' Louisa said, never once looking at the man and woman attending to her as they began their work. Each gently narrating what they were doing. Taking care until they finished.

One ambulance officer made way for him, and he took Louisa's hand. Small, pale. Cold. He wrapped his fingers round hers. Gave a gentle squeeze. It brought him back to the hospital visits with Felicity. How small and scared she was. The ever-present dread that the time he saw her would be the last, till his parents sent him away and the only things he had were vague reports begged from the people who should have loved him as much as they loved their own true daughter.

His gut twisted into sickening knots. The memories that came flooding back, of the flashing lights, the medical care, the fear. Like a nightmare that had gone on for years till the news had finally come that Flick was in remission. She'd stayed in remission ever since, yet each year on that date he waited for the call that would tell him the cancer had come back, even though she was now in her twenties with no signs of relapse, and his sister was considered cured. Still…

'Everything all right?' he asked.

'Blood pressure's a little low, heart rate's a little high. Lungs are clear. Otherwise, no injuries. We'd like her to stay here a little while, have some oxygen. Take her observations again.'

'Are you okay with that, Louisa? I can ask them to call me over when they want to look at you again. For now, I'd like to go and check on Mrs Fancutt and talk to the others.'

The column of her slender throat moved in a swallow. 'That's fine.'

He stood and strode to a small group, huddled near a fire engine under some hastily erected cover. The rain wasn't heavy any more but driven by the wind and stinging his bare legs as he held the blanket tight round him.

'Everyone okay here?' They all nodded, asked about him. Of Louisa especially.

'We're both fine.'

The housekeeper looked at him, her normally tidy grey hair a mess of being woken from sleep and the weather. 'Are you sure?'

'We have no injuries.'

'That's not what I meant. Miss Louisa hasn't been outside the house in months, other than to attend the funeral. She hasn't left the property other than to visit the village in far longer.'

Matteo stilled. He spent his time travelling, visiting his properties, working. He had 'homes' all over the world. His house in Italy when he'd sought to find his birth parents in earnest. The gleaming modern masterpiece of an apartment in New York, a chateau in the Loire Valley... He shook his head. Home was where he laid his head for the moment, not any one house or apartment.

'How long is "far longer"?'

Mrs Fancutt hesitated. 'Years.'

He stilled. What kind of life had she led? Louisa had talked about love but what held her here? He could hardly believe his great-aunt would compel her to stay. However, what did he know? This whole family was steeped in self-interest.

She needs to be looked after...

'Has she ever travelled? Been out of the country?'

'Never, though Mae, God rest her soul, did try. Even got her a passport. Used to tell Louisa of her adventures when she was a young woman. Encouraging her to go on her own. She never did.'

Matteo glanced over at the ambulance. No wonder Louisa was reluctant to leave Easton Hall. She didn't know what kind of world was out there waiting to be explored. With the money he was prepared to give her, she could do anything she wanted. An idea struck him. Louisa was trapped in an existence steeped in the past, yet she was a young woman with a big future in a wide world.

Whilst she might not believe him, he simply needed to show it to her.

Louisa sat in the back of a large black car. The luxury vehicle easing through the glaring, crowded streets of Milan. How could it have been only days since the storm and fire? That time had seemed to pass in a complete blur. All the while, Matteo had been there. Taking charge, taking control. Calmly talking to staff about what would happen until Easton Hall could be properly assessed. How their wages would be protected. Sourcing a replacement passport because hers was trapped in a house they couldn't now enter till it was deemed safe.

Then he'd simply told her she was coming with him, bundled her into a private jet and flown her to one of his luxury hotels in northern Italy.

She'd tried to marvel at the flight, her first. The sky, so vast. The clouds like spun sugar in the sky. Yet it was as if she were cut adrift, having lost everything safe and familiar. Sitting in the back of the ambulance had brought back memories, taking her to dark places she hadn't been in years. The nightmares she'd once suffered regularly, returning. Yet she didn't have her sketchbook with her to draw them when she woke, to take away their power.

She took a deep breath. The lack of her art things carried a greater worry, that she'd fall behind on her illustrations when she had a contract to fulfil. A deadline, and Louisa *never* missed those. She'd tried to explain that to Matteo as well, yet he'd simply waved away her concerns. Said that he'd look after her. Told her to have some time off and have fun, when Louisa was convinced they had different meanings for the word. Like today, when he'd arranged a personal stylist to come and take her to buy clothes, on his account. They'd sourced a few simple dresses in the UK before leaving, but, with everything else trapped in the house, even she could see that she needed more.

'Milan is the city of fashion,' he'd said, as if that meant

anything to her. The woman sitting next to her in the soft white leather seats seemed to understand the assignment. Elegant to a fault with glossy, smooth chocolate hair. A sharp black suit. Vibrant, multicoloured silk blouse with a stylishly asymmetrical bow at the neck. Barely there make-up. Long, manicured nails.

A picture of perfection, who'd seen Louisa, pursed her lips, looked her up and down. Then nodded once and simply said, 'Come with me.'

No conversation about what she might like. Nothing. Now Louisa's belly churned as if it were full of snakes. Why did she feel so…judged? Her needs were simple. Maybe Matteo had said something when arranging the day? Perhaps that he'd found her in some way lacking? Though why that should even matter, she couldn't be sure.

He was the enemy. Trying to take away her home. She shouldn't care less about what he thought of her. Should she?

They pulled up outside a building fronted with smooth cream marble. Windows of glistening glass. Gleaming gold accents. No name on the shopfront. A man in a dark suit opened the car door and she followed the stylist out into the harsh summer sunshine. The humidity of the day draped over Louisa like a damp blanket. Likely making her hair frizz, the floral cotton of her pretty dress crinkle and hang limp.

It didn't seem to affect the woman she was with, who still looked crisp and cool as though she'd just stepped from a freezer. Cutting her way through the throng of tourists on the footpath who parted in her wake, whereas Louisa felt hemmed in, pressed on all sides.

She scurried to catch up, dodging a couple who'd stopped in front of her to take photographs, as the stylist strode through the door of the shop. Dagger-sharp heels, clicking staccato on the marble flooring as she entered. Leading Louisa through the back to a kind of showroom with plush couches, champagne on ice and racks of vibrant clothes. A couple more perfectly presented women entered. Assessing her. She spied herself in a wall of mirrors. Long red hair curling at the ends. No make-up. Floral cotton dress. Ballet flats.

'Please take a seat.'

She was guided to a couch, handed a glass of champagne. Some strawberries. She didn't want the champagne right now, although the berries looked delicious. She put the glass down as a conversation in Italian swirled round her. Talking *about* her, she was sure. She bit into a strawberry and a burst of juice exploded from the luscious fruit, dripping onto her dress. Leaving a blot of pink on the fabric as she was being…studied.

'Can I please have a napkin and some water to clean this before it stains?'

'You won't need it. A man like Signor Bainbridge has certain…requirements for a woman and how she's dressed,' the woman said to her. Louisa wasn't sure of her name. They hadn't even really been introduced. She'd just swept in like a perfect, perfumed tidal wave and washed Louisa away with her.

'He does?' Louisa couldn't understand. Wasn't this trip about clothes for her? Why should Matteo care what she wore? Although he was paying, which didn't sit right, but that was another thing he simply waved off in his imperious kind of way.

'Of course. We will cater for all of them here. We have many ideas for you.'

What about her ideas for herself? She knew what she needed, what she wanted. What she liked. Though she supposed these people were professionals. She could sit back. At least it was cool here, out of the sunshine and the humidity.

They began taking clothes from the racks, holding them up for her. Suits as sharp as theirs. As sharp as Matteo's own. Black, a colour she swore she'd only wear to a funeral. Bejewelled dresses with plunging necklines. Crystal-covered stilettos when she'd never worn a pair in her life and would likely break a limb or her neck if she tried. Nothing looked like *her* or felt like her style, at all. She was happy to try something new, but this? She kept shaking her head as the assembled women's lips thinned, eyes narrowed, brows creased.

'What *do* you like to wear?' one of them asked.

She waved her hands up and down her body. 'Dresses a bit like this. I also wore vintage clothes at home. I felt… pretty in those.'

'And what if you were to go to a formal dinner? A cocktail party? Accompany Signor Bainbridge on a business lunch?'

'I—I'm a children's book illustrator. Why would I go to anything like that?'

They all muttered amongst themselves. Seemed to change tack. Out came underwear. Filmy lace. Embroidery. Barely there. Beautiful. But how would it even look on her and *why*? Something uncomfortable prickled at the back of her neck. A heated sensation that was part unpleasant and part sliding temptation. Did they think…?

'I'm not Matteo's lover.'

The women stopped their bustling. Stared at her.

'What does it matter what you are?' the stylist asked, one perfectly plucked brow raised. 'We must do *something* with you. Perhaps your hair. It's so…long. Cut. Highlights. Then you'll feel like a new woman and want clothes.'

It was as if a hand grabbed Louisa's throat and cut off her breath. She loathed the thought of anyone cutting her hair after her mother regularly had when she was a child, even taking to it with thinning scissors to reduce its thickness. To try and make her daughter look ill. Louisa had vowed that she'd *never* be subjected to that again. She stood, but the women completely ignored her. All nodded at the fine idea of changing her into someone else, and went back to talking amongst themselves.

The thing was, Louisa had accepted herself long ago. Mae and counselling had shown her that she was enough. And so, her mother's barbed comments had dimmed over time. Why wasn't she blonde, unfreckled, thinner, taller? Now, these women were a reminder of how others saw her. Tears burned the back of her nose. She didn't need to be turned into someone else because some strangers wanted to squeeze her into a box that didn't fit.

'No,' she said.

'Come dici?' the stylist asked.

Even though Louisa couldn't speak Italian the phrase was said in a way that clearly meant, *What on earth are you talking about?*

Louisa shook her head. Right now, she had to go. Today wasn't fun. It was another kind of nightmare.

'This is all a mistake. I won't wear those clothes. I refuse to cut my hair. I want to go back to the hotel. We're done here.'

CHAPTER FOUR

MATTEO STRODE INTO his suite. It had been a successful morning in all respects. Arriving in Milan, finalising the negotiations for another property. He shrugged off his jacket and tossed it onto a chair and loosened his tie. Undid the top button of his shirt. Rolled up his sleeves. It was only the afternoon—however, something had pulled him back here. He was keen to see how Louisa's own day had gone. The first step in showing her all she'd missed in life, living with Mae. What woman didn't love shopping for clothes? Milan was the perfect place to do that. Such a magnificent city with its combination of history mingled with modernity. Even though he'd anticipated her shopping trip would take most of the morning, perhaps she might have been able to do some sightseeing as well?

That thought piqued his interest—what she thought of her first foreign city. He glanced at the door that joined his suite to hers. Walked to it. Knocked. He was almost surprised when it opened, so he walked through.

Louisa faced away from him, staring out of the hotel windows onto Milan's rooftops. Hair tumbling down her back in glorious waves of red. Still wearing a floral dress from a small boutique in the village near Easton

Hall they'd managed to visit after the fire. Pretty, to be sure, but nothing like what she could find in this city. Though he was surprised the suite wasn't full of packages. He'd been clear that money was no object in the stylist's efforts. There was to be no impediment to securing anything Louisa wanted.

'How was your day?' he asked.

She turned. He expected a beaming smile. Strangely craved it, since Louisa hadn't smiled once since they'd met only days ago. What woman didn't deserve a little happiness after what she'd been through?

Except there was no smile. Her face a mask of almost forced neutrality.

'I couldn't find anything to wear.'

Impossible. He'd been explicit, and the stylist was an expert. Perhaps Louisa didn't want to spend his money, although he'd tried to reassure her that she needed clothes. A couple of dresses and one hauntingly sheer nightgown were not enough. Even Louisa could see that…

Then he noticed. Her eyes, rimmed pink. Her nose, a little pink too.

Had she been crying?

He took a step forward, then another till he was close. She looked up at him, her lips trembling at the corners a fraction. Eyes bright with what he feared were tears. A heat boiled in his gut. He'd expected smiles, not sadness. He tamped the rising anger down. Trying to get to the bottom of what had happened. People did what he asked, or they paid.

It seemed someone would be owing him today.

'Didn't you see anything you liked?'

As he looked down on her, Louisa's pupils flared wide. The green of her eyes seemingly more vibrant in this moment. Captivating, like the verdant grass round Easton Hall.

'They showed me things I'd never wear. I tried telling them but they…'

She bit her lip as she hesitated. Took a jagged breath.

'Tell me,' he said, his jaw clenching. The way her eyes tightened, her soft pink lips turned down… Clearly today hadn't been a good day.

'The way those women looked at me. They didn't make me feel beautiful. They wanted to cut my hair.'

A shudder tremored through her as a blaze of fury tore through his veins. Not beautiful? How could they not see? And how could *anyone* suggest cutting off her hair, that glorious river of fire? He couldn't comprehend it.

Moisture pooled in the corners of her eyes. No. This was *not* what he'd asked for or envisaged. He craved to reach out, hold. Soothe. But why? Seduction of innocents wasn't the game here. Showing her what she'd been missing out on in life was, and he'd failed. Spectacularly.

Failure wasn't part of his repertoire. Time to fix what others had clearly broken.

'You are beautiful. That's a fact and not open for discussion. As for your hair?' What he wouldn't give to plunge his hands into the thickness of it. Find out whether it was as silky as it appeared. 'Anyone who'd consider cutting it would be contemplating a *crime*.'

Her mouth opened a fraction, with a breathy inhale. 'They thought I was your lover. Said you had…expectations.'

His brain snagged on one word. *Lover.* The heat that had flared in his gut rushed low. How she'd felt in his arms when he carried her from Easton Hall. The soft weight of her against his naked torso. What if they had been lovers? He'd carry her to this bed like that. Her head thrown back in ecstasy as her green eyes glazed in passion. Hair spilled like blood across his pillow. He could count every freckle on her body. Kiss each one...

No. He almost shook his head to rid his mind of the intoxicating fog of those imaginings. Innocents weren't for him. He'd been focussed on business for too long, that was all. What with investigating the Bainbridge family's charities' interests for fraud and then planning his quest for revenge, he hadn't been with a woman for some time. No wonder he was reacting like an eighteen-year-old with no control over his own body.

He took a step back. Turned round. Clenched his fists and willed his inconvenient arousal away.

'The *only* expectation I had was that you'd find clothes that you liked. My error was the choice of stylist, which I'll rectify immediately.'

She gave a shaky laugh. 'Not those women again, they didn't like me much.'

They weren't paid to like her. They were paid to do their job. To ensure she felt beautiful and cherished, and to make the whole process fun. The failure of his mission quelled his remaining desire like being doused in chilled water. He turned back round to face her. Noticing how...worn she seemed.

'She needs to be looked after...'

'Have you eaten?' he asked.

She shook her head. 'I kind of lost my appetite after being told something needed to be *done* with me.'

How *dared* they.

'If you had an appetite, what would you like?'

'A cheese toastie.'

He picked up his phone, ordered one for each of them. Whilst it wasn't something traditionally on the room service menu here, he had no doubt the hotel chef would make the best damned cheese toastie Louisa had ever eaten.

'Food first, shopping next.'

One of her hands gripped the fabric of her dress, twisting it in her fingers. 'I'm not keen to relive the experience.'

'You'll enjoy this, I promise you.'

Matteo was intent on recovering the day. A few phone calls later and he'd spoken to another woman. One he'd been assured could help him. She seemed more than amenable to dropping everything to search out suitable clothes and deliver them to his hotel. She asked about Louisa's style, and for a photograph of her, which he promised to send. 'Country look, cottage core,' she'd suggested. He didn't understand what that meant but it didn't matter. This time, he'd stay to supervise the process.

Failure was *not* an option.

Louisa didn't want to go back to more clothes shopping, but she was powerless to resist. How had she not recognised what a force of nature Matteo was? He'd simply stormed into the room and taken over. Whilst she couldn't understand the Italian he'd been speaking on the phone; his voice had been terse. Command and authority. All for her. Something about it had been...electrifying. To watch him work, take charge. She could imagine mere mortals simply rolling over and doing his bidding with no fight at all.

Was that what he'd expected of her, when he'd said he wanted her out of Easton Hall?

She couldn't think of that right now. As much as she'd stood up for herself earlier in the day, the cold words of three impeccably styled women had still taken their toll. She'd felt old-fashioned. Unattractive. Past insecurities calling to her in their nasty but seductive voices. Yet when she'd told Matteo…

He thought she was beautiful.

What did he say? That it was a fact *'not open for discussion'*. And she realised he was the first man other than her father to say that about her. With his words it was as if she basked in the warm, golden glow of spring sunshine. Though she shouldn't, Louisa found his approval hard to resist even though his aims and hers weren't aligned.

'How was your toastie?' he asked.

A perfect concoction of crisp buttery bread, melting cheese and the bite of mustard. 'I've never tasted better.'

The corner of Matteo's lips quirked. 'I'm sure the chef would like to hear that.'

'Do you always stay in your hotels, or do you have a home base anywhere?'

This place was a masterpiece of elegance with warm earth tones, jewelled accents, and sleek modern styling. The freestanding bath was almost like a swimming pool, with a chandelier above it that had made her feel like royalty as she'd wallowed in the tub. Everything a picture of sheer opulence. Yet she couldn't imagine this was where he spent all his time, though why she held that unshakable view she couldn't really say. It just seemed the hotel was somewhere he'd created for others, not himself.

'I have lots of places to live,' he said, arms out wide. 'Take your pick of country. Italy, France, the US.'

'Are they all your *homes*?'

He cocked his head to the side. A tiny frown creased his brow. 'I own them. I stay there. Isn't that enough?'

She shook her head.

'Not where you sleep. I'm talking about somewhere where you're happy to be. Every time you walk through the door, it's a relief. Your safe space, the one that holds your fondest memories. The place that you can be entirely yourself?'

That was what Easton Hall had been to her. A sanctuary. She'd spent so long feeling as though she'd had to hide, with people not listening to her. There, she could be who she was without any question. Today out in Milan had simply reaffirmed what she'd always thought: Easton Hall was her place. Where she fitted, like the final piece slotted into a puzzle.

Matteo's eyes widened, then he frowned. 'That's not what a home means. It's a place to stay.'

That was why he thought paying her off would convince her to leave Easton Hall. How could she ever convince someone who didn't understand the true meaning of home how important a real home was to her?

Before she could carry on the conversation his phone buzzed an alert.

'Ahh. I promised food then clothes. The clothes have arrived.'

The delicious toastie in her stomach seemed to have congealed to a solid rock in an instant. She took a deep breath, steeling herself for more judgement and humiliation.

A gentle knock sounded at the door and Matteo opened it. In walked a woman, once again with impeccable style. Though not sharp in black and bold colours but somehow more accessible in pale grey trousers, a soft cream blouse, and pastel-coloured scarf casually tossed round her throat. She shook Matteo's hand, her whole demeanour businesslike. Louisa stood and the woman turned, a wide and warm smile on her face. Introduced herself as Sylvana. Directed a couple of men with clothing racks into the suite. Louisa scanned the racks and her shoulders dropped a fraction, relaxing. No black to be seen.

'I hope you like what I have to show you. Please take a seat and we'll go through what I've found.'

Louisa glanced at Matteo. Was he going to stay? She guessed so, the way he'd sprawled on the lounge like a panther making itself comfortable in the sun. She sat in an armchair as Sylvana took dress after dress from the racks. All breathtakingly beautiful. Some she wouldn't wear, many she would. The woman reorganised the racks into the clothes Louisa might like and the clothes she didn't.

All the while Matteo watched, staring at the selections, then looking at her. What was he thinking? Imagining her in the clothes, wondering whether they'd suit her? The man was inscrutable, even though the awareness of his gaze brushed over her like the soft, expensive fabrics Sylvana invited her to touch to ensure she liked the feel of them against her skin.

'I hear that your house recently caught fire, which

is why you have no clothes,' Sylvana said, with a look of real concern on her face as she began wheeling the clothes rack with Louisa's selections into the bedroom. 'I'm sorry. But let's start the fun by trying these clothes on.'

'I'm not sure this is my idea of fun,' Louisa said. 'I usually wear vintage day dresses that I found in the attic in my old home.'

Sylvana put her hand to her chest. 'Oh, *davvero*? I studied fashion history here in Milan. Those pieces would be irreplaceable. Were they lost in the fire?'

Louisa shrugged, rubbing at the tight ache in her chest even contemplating the loss. 'I don't know. Maybe. The fire was put out quickly, but no one can go into the house right now.'

'*È terribile!* Let's hope, then. This is at least a beginning. Not vintage masterpieces, but something I think you'll be comfortable in.'

She tried on the clothes. Not vintage, as Sylvana said, but dresses that still made her feel a little like a princess. With skirts that twirled as she spun round in them, big sleeves, glorious colours of greens, blues and pinks. Brighter, bolder than normal.

'You should show Signor Bainbridge,' Sylvana said.

Louisa's heart seemed to do a little twirl of its own in her chest at that suggestion. 'Really?'

'He's a man who stays, so he must want to see. Go,' the woman said, with a shooing motion of her hands.

Louisa peeked round the open bedroom door. Matteo still lounged on the couch, phone in hand. Shirtsleeves rolled up showing his strong, tanned forearms. He noticed her in mere seconds, lifted his head. She felt almost silly. What did she know about men's...wants? Surely he couldn't care less about the clothes she wore?

'You are beautiful. That's a fact and not open for discussion.'

'Sylvana said you might like to see one of the dresses?'

He put down his phone on the couch next to him, removed his tie. Her gaze fixed on the slice of brown skin at his throat, the hint of hair on his chest.

'Of course.'

She hesitated a moment before stepping out of the bedroom, brushing her hands down the skirt of fabric patterned with large royal-blue flowers. Did a little pirouette because she wasn't sure what else she was supposed to do, this was all so new for her. The full skirt swayed round her legs.

'Perfetto,' Matteo murmured, his voice deep. Rumbling right through her. Suddenly it was as if she'd run a mile. The way her heart thrummed. Her breath catching in her chest.

'Would you like to see another?'

His lips curled into a slow, appreciative smile. The type of smile that could make a woman lose all sense. 'What do you think?'

Heat flared to her cheeks. 'Okay. Yes.'

She ran back to the bedroom, put on another dress. This one in autumn colours with a ruffle at the neckline and tiers in the skirt that went down to her ankles. Sylvana smiled, handed her a straw hat. 'Wear it with this.'

She placed the hat on her head, trying not to run back into the room to show Matteo. Instead, she took a deep breath, counted to five and then attempted to stroll. As she left the bedroom, she noticed that he wasn't on his phone again. It was as if he'd been waiting for her. His eyes, heavy lidded. His lips parted. She did another twirl. 'What do you think of this one?'

'*Bellissima.*'

Didn't that word mean beautiful? His voice was rough, a rasp. A shiver of pleasure at the sound shimmied up her spine. She was intoxicated by his approval, giddy with it. This was wrong. He wanted to take away her home. Yet why did it seem so right? No, it meant nothing. It was simply the moment, that was all. She'd had an awful morning, he'd been kind. And what woman wouldn't want to be told she was beautiful by a man who looked like a bronzed god? Yet…his gaze raked over her, golden brown eyes molten. Then he leaned forwards, hands clasped in front of him. As though he wanted to get closer to her somehow, except was holding himself back.

Awareness shimmered over her, the sparkle of goosebumps. Time slowed syrupy and sweet. And whilst she'd listened to his words, with the heat in his gaze she began to believe them. She might have felt like a princess before, but the way he looked at her right now?

It made Louisa feel like a goddess.

Matteo sat back on the plush sofa as Louisa almost skipped back into the bedroom. Her dress of golden tones had matched her hair. With the straw hat on her head and freckles dusting her nose and upper chest, she looked like the embodiment of summer. He couldn't wait for the next change because this was a plan working. What he'd hoped for. Louisa was having fun.

She almost bounded out of the bedroom this time, in a

dress of pinks and oranges. The hem ruffled. Shorter at the front, longer at the back. The neckline a little deeper than the others, nestling in her cleavage. Myriad tiny buttons down the front that any red-blooded man would crave to undo, slowly. To unwrap the prize of her gentle curves, to see if those freckles he'd observed earlier covered her whole body.

She stopped in front of him, not moving. Waiting. Feet bare. Matteo wasn't sure why the ability to see her toes struck him as so intensely intimate. Ridiculous. He lifted his hand, twisted his finger in a circle, and she twirled for him. Arms out, hair spilling wild round her as the hem of her dress swished about her calves. A smile broke free on her face, then she laughed. It burst through him bright and joyous as the first rays of sunrise over the horizon. There were no words to adequately describe how she looked in this moment, so he didn't try.

'I think you might enjoy shopping after all.'

It was as if a little light died. Cloud passing over the sun. Louisa worried her bottom lip in her teeth again, as if her insecurities had returned. 'I—I didn't enjoy the city or the stores, but this was fun. Yes.'

Something about the scene gave him pause. Milan had been an error. He'd brought her to a busy metropolis when she'd spent her formative years in the country. This hotel, a marvel of modernity in a bustling city, didn't fit Louisa. There were so many other areas of Italy he could see her enjoying more. Matteo didn't want her overwhelmed, he wanted her…overcome. With the beauty and wonder of new places, so she'd see that life at Easton Hall had been a trap, holding her back.

She'd asked him earlier whether he had a home base.

That wasn't a concept he understood. He hadn't even felt as if he'd had a home as a child, being shunted to boarding school, not wanted by his adoptive parents. Everywhere only temporary. However, there *was* one place that was closer to Louisa's description than the rest. The first house he'd ever purchased, when he'd discovered his heritage was Italian. A place he'd taken no one before.

A place where he hoped Louisa would finally grow her wings and fly.

CHAPTER FIVE

LOUISA WATCHED AS the landscape slid by through the car's tinted window. Matteo had told her he had some surprises for her, then organised for their belongings to be packed, bundled her into another luxury vehicle and they'd exited his hotel, leaving the bustle of Milan behind them. Whilst she'd admired that he'd been a man of action in the days earlier, she was a little tired of being... bundled. Some hints might have been nice, minus the arrogance of Matteo's certainty that she'd like what he had in mind.

Though she did rather enjoy this. They'd left the city and headed north, so she'd been told. Now, their car travelled along a narrow road bordered on one side by houses, stone walls and greenery, and on the other, a vivid blue lake before a backdrop of mountains. It was vast. Take-your-breath-away beautiful. The sunshine sparkling on the water, little boats dotting the surface.

Lake Como, he'd told her as the water had first come into view. At least he'd finally told her *something*.

Though talk about take your breath away... She dragged her gaze from the view to glance at Matteo, sitting next to her. Looking effortlessly casual in navy-coloured chinos and a white polo shirt that only accentuated the warm brown of his skin. A large golden watch gleaming at his wrist. He was talking on his phone again. Giving instructions in Italian. She wondered where he'd learned the language so fluently, and why. Another question that she wondered whether he'd give her an answer to. Even though he never seemed to stop working, he looked well rested, as though he had no worries in the world.

As if it were his to rule. When she still wasn't sure some days why life was so chaotic and hard.

Oddly her life seemed a little less chaotic and hard now that Matteo was in it. Which was difficult to understand when he wanted to evict her from her home. She could refuse him. Say she was going to stay. Though she wasn't sure how that would work, since the place was currently unliveable…

'Where are we going to this time?' she asked as the unfamiliar countryside flew past.

'My villa.'

A tiny thrill ran through her. What would one of his houses be like? A modern masterpiece or something else? She'd noticed a subtle change in him as they'd travelled. He seemed more relaxed now, something about him less hard, more…fluid. Such a presence about him, he filled the cabin of the car with it. In this enclosed space the scent of him was like walking through some heady spice market. It scrambled her senses.

Then Matteo smiled and *that* smile reached his eyes, the corners crinkling as if he was truly happy. In that moment, she could barely breathe.

'You'll enjoy it,' he said. 'I promise.'

Promises were fraught things. They led to so much

expectation yet often failed on delivery. Bitter experience with her mother had taught her not to believe in them.

'Isn't there a quote, promises were made to be broken?'

'I don't break mine.' It was said as a fact she should simply accept. 'And I told you I have a few surprises for you when we get there.'

He didn't say anything more, yet the faint, self-satisfied smile on his face as they reached an ornate iron gate, which opened before them like magic, told her that he was pretty pleased with himself.

The car's tyres crunched on a gravel drive that followed the lake. Soon, they pulled up outside a magnificent two-storey villa, painted a warm ochre with blue-shuttered windows. The gardens surrounding were clipped and restrained, unlike the wild tangle of Easton Hall. Yet whilst it was all so unfamiliar, something about the surrounds eased a tension inside her. It was as if her whole body could let out a sigh. The privacy of it all. Expansive lake on one side, tree-covered hills to the other.

He opened the door of the car, got out. She followed.

'Home sweet home,' she said.

'As I've said before, I don't have a home. Not as you define it. This is a convenient base when I have to take care of business in Italy.'

'Then why have it at all?'

'It was good value.' He shrugged his broad, strong shoulders. 'I contemplated turning it into one of my hotels.'

He led her towards the front door of the villa. She took a moment to stop, look out over the gardens terraced down to the lake beyond. Sucked in a deep breath.

The air here was warmer than home. Scented with jasmine and citrus blossom. To the right of the door sat a plaque: Villa Arcadia.

Arcadia was the name of his hotel chains.

'Which came first?' she asked, nodding to the sign. 'The house or the hotels?'

Something triggered in the back of her brain. Arcadia meant something. Louisa couldn't remember what. She'd have to look it up.

'The house. It's the first I ever purchased.'

He unlocked the door and led her inside to an entrance hall with a marble floor topped with a Persian carpet runner. Furniture, the warm honey of polished antiques.

'Why nowhere in the UK?' she asked. She would have thought his first property purchase would have been there.

'I have an affinity here. My heritage is Italian.'

That admission surprised her. 'How do you know?'

Back when she was young, her mother used to speak of the benevolence of Matteo's adoptive parents. How they'd taken in a foundling as their own, as if it was some great charity. Yet in her family's eyes, it hadn't made him a true Bainbridge.

'Family history DNA.' He shut the front door behind him and all of him seemed to shut down too, close off with the clear warning that this wasn't something he wanted to talk about, so she didn't press.

'I thought you'd want to see your surprises,' he said. 'Come with me.'

Matteo gave her an encouraging smile to accompany the deft change of subject, focussing on her once more. Another smile that didn't reach his eyes. He showed her through the house, in many ways like his hotels with its neutral colours. Bright with sunlight in every room. Yet this place was burnished with age. The eclectic combination of antiques with modern touches giving the villa an elegantly casual nudge into the present, which strangely felt like him.

'I-it's beautiful.'

Most rooms she saw opened onto a view of gardens or the lake, with expanses of glass. There was simply no place for any darkness here.

'Thank you. I hope you'll enjoy it.'

He led her up an internal staircase to the second floor, down another corridor, to a closed door.

'This is your room,' he said with almost a flourish as he pushed the door open and she walked inside.

Louisa took a few moments, scanning the space. The room had another glorious view of the lake but that wasn't what held her attention. The space disoriented her because, whilst there was a different view outside, the inside seemed achingly familiar. Her heart stuttered.

It was almost as if her room at Easton Hall had been lifted complete and placed here. Her bed. The rocking chair in the corner that used to be her father's. The rug on the floor. The paintings on the walls. *Everything*, down to the sketch pad and pens on the bedside table. Matteo stood at the door, head cocked to the side. Watching her. Not as if she were someone strange. But with a look on his face that was softer than she'd seen before.

Her heart filled with something warm and bright as the sunshine outside. A sensation gifting her that most cherished of feelings, *hope*, that in the mess of all of this, something could go right for once.

She didn't know what to do, what to say. It overwhelmed her. Instead, she ran to Matteo and simply hurled herself into him. He caught her with an 'oof' and then his strong arms wrapped round her. Keeping her together. Keeping her safe. Like the night he'd carried her out of Easton Hall when she'd been too paralysed to move.

Tears prickled her eyes.

'Thank you. It's everything I could have wanted,' she said, her voice cracking. Burying her face into his muscular chest. His heart thumping a steady, comforting beat. Other things came to her awareness. How solid he was. The heat and muscle of him. His stance didn't change, but something about him relaxed into her. The way they began meld together. His hands loosely stroking up and down her spine. She breathed him in, the scent of freshly laundered clothes and the spicy scent she'd begun to associate with him in the car...

She craved to simply absorb him into her. Have him fill every empty space. Her nipples tightened in her bra. Heat built between her legs. Naked want became like a living thing. Grabbing her by the throat, leaving her breathless. He shifted his legs, spread them a little wider, his hand on her back drifting a little lower before stopping. He loosened his arms, and she looked up at him, tears pooling in her eyes. Not caring that he could see the emotion.

'You can't know what this means to me.'

'I wanted to make you feel at home.'

His eyelids were hooded, golden brown eyes almost drowned out by his fathomless pupils. His lashes, impossibly long. Stubble darkening his angular jaw. Matteo's lips parted as if trying to get more air, then his gaze flicked. To her eyes, lips, throat. His Adam's apple bobbed in a swallow.

She wished she could be the sort of woman who'd know what to do here, rather than a person who sketched her fantasies instead of acting them out for real. If she were the type of person who took chances, she might get up on her toes and press her lips to his. But chances meant risk and risk had ceased to have any part in her life, long ago.

She tried to give him a happy smile, which halted with the merest of frowns creasing his brow as she stepped back from his embrace. Trying to pretend that nothing had happened, when it was as if the world had tilted on its axis.

'How did you manage it? I thought we couldn't go into the house.'

'You'd be surprised what I'm able to do,' he said.

She wasn't, not now. Louisa thought he could achieve just about anything he put his mind to. Somewhere in the far reaches of her consciousness that realisation sounded a prickle of warning, but she was too overcome to pay it any attention.

'I heard you talking to the stylist about your clothes. I'm having them professionally cleaned. The soft furnishings were smoke damaged, but I requested as close a facsimile as I could get for your room here.'

'I-it's very kind of you.' What more could she say? She was completely overcome by the thought and his generosity.

He shrugged. 'It's okay.'

The unmoved expression on his face told her he thought it was nothing.

'You don't understand.' She shook her head. How to make him see that this meant something more? 'It shows that you thought of me. For so many years, people only thought of themselves. This is rare, because in my life not many people have been kind.'

Kind? He wasn't kind. Other words were routinely used to describe him. Business magazines called him driven. His opposition called him ruthless. Women he dated might have called him focussed during the early stages, then remote just before their fling inevitably ended. He was a man who got what he wanted, and one word *never* used to describe him was kind.

He'd brought her things to Italy for his own ends because he wanted her comfortable. *Comfortable* was the place where he would encourage her to relinquish her right to reside. She'd see a world not to fear, but to explore. Why would she ever want to go back to Easton Hall after that?

Matteo turned and walked to the window, placing his hands on the ledge, pretending to look at the magnificent view he never really had the time to stop and take in anymore. Willing himself not to turn round, take Louisa into his arms again. Kiss her. He almost laughed. A *kind* man wouldn't be thinking those thoughts.

It had been another moment with Louisa in his arms. The softness of her body. The curves. The warmth. With another woman, he might explore the situation. But he was no fool. There was no way she could be anything other than entirely innocent. Whilst he was all for something more casual, for a woman like her with sex would come love. They walked hand in hand, which was why in the past he'd only dated woman with the same sense of world-weariness as himself. Women who knew what they wanted, took it when offered, and walked away. This was a woman who'd want romance and gentle words, seduction and softness. Eliciting her sighs of pleasure. They'd be the sweetest of music...

Why was he even thinking of that? None of these things were for him. He didn't do romance. He certainly didn't do love. He didn't know what it was. His childhood had proven to him that it didn't exist.

Those thoughts were enough to crush any desire right out of him. He realised long ago that his sole purpose in life was to succeed *despite* his family, to exact his revenge of taking their most prized possession. His success was the only thing that made people want him. Buzzing about like bees to the wealthy honeypot. It was how it had always been, people wanting him, not for who he was, the orphaned boy, but what he could provide them. For his parents, being an heir until his sister was born and he was cast aside. As for others, it was all about his power, his position. At least people were transparent that way. No longer would anyone fool him into believing they wanted Matteo Bainbridge the *man*. It was easier to know they wanted him for material things. Life was predictable then. There were no cruel surprises.

Matteo took a deep breath. He couldn't stare out of the window indefinitely. There was more he needed to show her. He turned round and Louisa was looking about the room. For the first time since leaving Easton Hall she seemed calmer. All of her, smoothed out. A slight smile on her face as her gaze fell on all of her familiar things. He wanted her to look at him again as if he was a man who could solve all her problems. There was something gratifying about it, something that stroked an ego he didn't even realise was important to him. If it could get him what he wanted in the end? All the better.

'There's more to show you,' he said.

'More? Haven't you done enough with this?'

She swept her arms wide around the room. This was nothing. Paying an engineer to urgently assess the living spaces of Easton Hall to safely allow people to collect her things. Hiring a team of interior decorators to find what matched the items that were smoke-and-water-damaged, fit everything in. Sure, he might have told them what room he thought suited best in the villa. The one with the finest view because Lake Como was beautiful at this time of the year.

But it happened because of his money, for no other reason.

Sadly, she didn't seem to want the money to leave Easton Hall. That would change. It always did. He just had to find the right price.

'I want to make sure you have what you need here,' he said. 'It's downstairs this time.'

She laughed and it was a joyous sound, like bird-song in the early morning. 'Why didn't you show me that first?'

'I thought you'd want to know where you were sleeping. That seems important to you.'

The smile on her face dimmed a little, all of her becoming more contemplative. 'So few people understand.'

He didn't. Not at all. Still, he could pretend.

But the thought of that pretence made something in his chest tighten. He rubbed at it, a strange kind of ache. Because in this moment he *wanted* to understand what made someone desire a place, a sense of belonging. Wanted to understand the woman.

Something about Louisa fascinated him. With so much hidden he was almost compelled to unravel all her secrets. What made a young woman stay in a home caring for her older relative? Eschew everything that appeared to signify modern style? Over the past years, working most days and rarely taking a break, he seemed to have lost his curiosity. Every interaction was one of problem and solution. Week after week, always on the move, putting out spot fires. With Louisa, he had the overwhelming desire to simply stop and learn more.

In the past, that curiosity had been dangerous.

'Do you want to know why you don't look like your parents?'

His whole life Matteo had been surrounded by people with blonde hair, pale skin and glacial blue eyes. He'd never really thought about why his skin tanned in the sun or his eyes were brown until his older cousin had pointed it out.

Then, he'd wanted to know.

'You're a fake.'

Curiosity killed the cat…

He'd approached his parents and that day they'd told him the truth. That he was adopted, but it didn't make any difference. Until Felicity came along and fell ill. Then their lies were exposed.

Yet his adoption was old news. Not something he needed to think about any more. Being curious about

Louisa would never be a bad thing. If he learned more, he could work out how to get her to leave Easton Hall.

All he needed was the right trigger point.

He almost looked forward to seeing how the game would play out between them. Whether he could coax anything more than the occasional whisper of pink on her cheeks from her. She seemed so…restrained. Then a vision flashed into his head of his fingers running through her glorious red hair, gripping it, drawing her head back to expose her perfect pale neck…

No. He needed to remind his errant body that seduction wasn't the game here. He was simply reacting to a beautiful woman unlike anyone he'd ever met before. It was the novelty of her.

Novelties always wore off.

'Come with me,' he said, motioning out of the door of her room.

They went back down the stairs, Louisa walking beside him in one of the dresses she'd modelled for him a couple of days earlier. It gave him a strange sense of satisfaction to see her wearing what he'd provided for her. To know that she liked it.

'I can see why you have an affinity for this place,' she said. 'I think it would be easy to love.'

There was that word again. Love. He didn't understand it.

'The UK's never seemed like home to me.'

'Why?'

What admission could he make that didn't damn him? The adopted child, unwanted by his birth mother. Unwanted by his adoptive family. What did that make him? Better to talk about what he could answer.

'When I found out I had Italian heritage, I visited here.'

To see if he could find any hint of the family he'd been sure was out there, somewhere, even though the DNA testing had turned up no relatives. It was as if his birth mother, father, had dissolved into the past as though they'd never existed. He was the only evidence that they'd lived at all. In the end he had himself, and that was what mattered.

Except he now had responsibility for Louisa too…

She looked over at him. 'And you felt something.'

'Yes.'

'If it were me, I'd say it felt like I'd come home.'

Was that right? It couldn't be. He hadn't wanted or needed a home in years, and it was freeing.

'No. Here was a place to start.'

Italy was the country of firsts. This property, his first boutique hotel. Milestones of his success. That was all.

'Have you ever looked for your birth family?'

'A little.'

A lie. He'd paid a small fortune to a well-regarded investigator, without success. Matteo needed to shut the conversation down. He didn't do this, the sharing. It was meaningless, reminding him of all that was wrong in his life rather than focussing on the important things, like moving forwards. Like the anticipation of showing Louisa the next room he had for her. Perhaps receiving another hug. Though how much better would a kiss be? Would…*more* be…?

'Did you find them?'

Louisa had stopped so he did too. He looked at her, face soft, full of what he feared was *empathy* when she shouldn't really care. No one else ever had. His throat tightened. Matteo shook his head.

'My birth parents? I've accepted I never will.'

She reached out, not with an exuberant full body hug, but with her hand. Touched his forearm, squeezed. Her grip surprisingly strong. He'd always thought of her as so small and fragile, yet he was beginning to think he might have underestimated her.

'I'm sorry, that must be difficult if you've wanted to meet them. Especially if you and your family...'

Her hand was hot on his forearm, burning like a brand. He pulled his arm away. Louisa rubbed her palm with her thumb. Her mouth slightly open. Those moss-green eyes of hers looking at him, as if deep into his soul. He didn't like that look, or what she might find there if she searched hard enough.

'I accept my life. It doesn't bother me. Anyhow, this isn't about me, it's about you.'

He smiled, but there was no pleasure in it. The type of smile he'd cultivated to use in business, one that did the job with no emotion underpinning it.

'O-okay.'

Louisa seemed hesitant as he led her to another room he'd chosen, one that had been an informal lounge. Large French doors leading out onto a paved terrace, decorated with pots of citrus trees, lavender and flowers. One of the best views of the lake from the bottom floor.

As Louisa walked in her gaze turned straight to the corner. Instead of flinging herself into his arms, she ran over to it. Her art desk, where she did her illustrations.

'Her work's really something.'

That was what one of his contractors had said, after

they'd called him to report successfully moving her things. The jealousy that had spiked through him at those words, when *he'd* never seen her pictures, was like a knife to his belly. He wanted her to offer. To show him. Yet she didn't say anything other than to check through the sketchbooks, as if cataloguing whether anything was missing. Louisa opened a drawer, peered inside the desk. Rummaged through everything with gentle, almost reverent hands.

'It's all here.'

'I should hope so. When I ask people to do a job, they do it.'

There was no excitement this time. Not like upstairs. He didn't know why that disappointed him, or what he'd really expected. She walked over to the doors leading to the patio. Tested one almost as if she wanted to escape, but it was locked. The light shone in from outside, and she was backlit, the skirt of her dress becoming sheer, her legs silhouetted like a soft pastel smudge through the fabric.

She said nothing, just looked out at the lake.

'I hope you're happy. I know how important the deadline is to you.'

Louisa reached up her hand to her face as if brushing something away. Then she turned. Her smile was a tremulous, fragile thing. Her eyes a little red, gleaming with tears. It was like a gut punch, striking all the air from him. He started forwards.

'Louisa.'

Like a few days before, he wasn't sure why the reaction to her tears was such a visceral thing. As he moved closer, he wanted to take her into his arms, wrap her tight and soothe those tears away. He could. It wouldn't take much. A few steps.

Instead, he stayed right where he was.

'Thank you, I...' She took a deep breath, her shoulders rising and falling. 'Your thoughtfulness... In my life... nothing's ever really felt like it was about me.'

'That's not fair.'

'Life's not fair.'

The words carried so much weight. A heaviness falling across everything. Of course, both her parents had died, leaving her in the care of Mae, who, in the end, she'd had to care for too. 'No, it isn't.'

She nodded, then turned back to the scene in front of her. This was one of his favourite rooms in the house. He hoped she liked it too.

'It's perfect. I couldn't have asked for more in the circumstances.'

That was his reminder. He had a job to do, to convince her to leave Easton Hall. To fight off the family too, who were still making noises about challenging the will...

'The world's a beautiful place.' He had hotels and retreats in some of the most sought-after places on the planet. 'Venice, with its spectacular arched bridges and canals. Jaipur, the Pink City. Or the Whitsundays, with some of the most exquisite beaches in the world. I've been almost everywhere.'

'I've never been to the beach.'

She said it quietly, almost as if it was some terrible admission. He couldn't fathom it, not ever having seen the ocean. Not having travelled. Why hadn't Mae pushed her harder? He gritted his teeth. Instead, Louisa was hidden away when there was a whole world to explore. If she was afraid to go on her own, he could show it all to her. The bright lights of New York, in the city that never slept. The pyramids of Egypt, with all their history. The beauty of Paris, the romance…

Why was he thinking of romance? Never once had thoughts of it entered his head before, not even when he'd bought his first hotel there. It was simply another place to stay in his nomadic life.

'I have a beach here. On the lake. There are a few public ones but mine's private. It might not be the ocean, but I can show you if you like? We could go there now.'

He wanted that look on her face again, of joy. Her laughter.

She smiled. It was a fragile, tremulous kind of thing. 'I'd like that. Maybe a bit later? I want to set up my work-space first. Make a start. I—I've never missed a deadline before, and I'd like to get back on track.'

His gut clenched, almost like disappointment. Though why he should have any sense of that was beyond him. He had work to do. Another brief report from the struc-tural engineer to read about Easton Hall. Insurance claims to consider. After that, he'd take her to the lake. They could treat this like a holiday for her, a grand ad-venture. Then she'd see that returning to live in a mould-ering old stately home in the country was a complete waste. That there was a world to see and he'd pay her very well to allow her the means of doing so. If she trav-elled, she could stay at any one of his retreats or hotels, then he'd know she was safe and looked after. He'd be fulfilling his promise to Mae.

It all made complete sense. Though he wasn't sure why the bile rose bitter in his throat, thinking of it all.

'How long do you need?'

'A couple of hours?'

She walked back to her desk. To the brushes and the sketchbooks. Her paints. There, he witnessed a look. It was difficult to define. Something like true happiness.

Had he ever found anything like it in his work? It was more a means to an end. Something he was good at. Was it his passion?

Matteo wasn't sure. What he did drove him every day. He'd done better than he'd ever believed possible when he'd first started out. Was known around the world as providing the finest luxury retreats and hotels where privacy and comfort reigned. A home away from home only…better.

And what made him the best of the best were his drive and perfectionism. He rarely had a day away from it. Allowed himself no distractions. Yet Louisa seemed to be occupying more and more of his thinking time. Easton Hall he could understand, given that was part of his plan, yet that place and Louisa were inextricably bound. He needed to keep his eyes on the prize, finally wrestling the home away from the clutches of his family and into his business. The ultimate win.

He watched Louisa getting to work. Today, her hair was bound in a long plait down her back. How he longed to see it loose again, spilling long and red in its perfect copper waves.

Later.

'I'll be back in two hours, then,' he said, before walking to the door. Already, Louisa had begun immersing herself in her work. She'd slipped on reading glasses. The first time he'd seen her in them since the day he'd arrived at Easton Hall. They made her look…cute. Almost studious. Another side to her that he craved to explore.

He shook his head. No. She was a distraction he needed to ignore.

Yet why did leaving the room seem like one of the hardest things he'd ever done?

CHAPTER SIX

ON HER BEST days Louisa would fall into the rhythm of her illustrations. The scratch of the ink pen on the page. The flow of the watercolour washes, the coloured pencils. Today, though, something was different. It was as if the sunlight in Italy changed her drawings. The brightness of it all. Everything vibrant and glowing. Her colours more saturated. She pushed her glasses up her nose. On her page sat another frog prince roughly sketched out in ink. Never without his jaunty smirk, because that was his signature. Hopping about with his crown askew on his head. She smiled. Her characters often took on a life of their own. She added a few sprigs of lavender to the foreground. A lake in the midground. Castle and mountains in the distance.

Could she incorporate the evolution of her drawings into the story? Start the colours softer and, as the story went on, let them increase in vibrancy?

It was unlike her normal style, but it was an idea.

Something about the freshness of it all excited her. Whilst she loved her work it had been a while since the creativity had given her the kind of squirming thrill in her belly when things just *worked*. She added a few butterflies to her sketch. Bright little bursts of colour. Like the butterflies flitting about in her stomach right now, bouncing about like popping candy. Though that might have less to do with her drawing and more with something else.

Matteo was going to show her a *beach*.

She'd seen them in photographs, of course, as a teenager when scouring the vast library of Easton Hall. So many glorious books, most age appropriate and some, well, not so much. Great-Uncle Gerald had had a diverse collection and she'd found quite a stash of erotica when she'd gone searching. She looked over at the beige covered sketchbook in her pile containing the drawings she did, just for herself. Her nightmares so they lost their hold. Her fantasies. The pictures no one would ever see…

A sharp knock sounded at the door, and she jumped. Those butterflies in her belly flapping about as if caught in a strong gust of wind.

'Come in.'

Matteo sauntered inside and her breath hitched. He'd changed into something more casual. Shorts, showing his legs. The strong calves sprinkled with dark hair. Another polo shirt that gripped him in all the right places. The whole of her flushed hot. She was sure that she'd gone a bright shade of pink, and that realisation made her skin burn even hotter.

She'd never really noticed men before. There were men who worked on the estate, but most of them had been with Mae for years and were much older. There was a young man in the grocer's in the village who had a nice smile when she walked through the door. But he didn't make her blush. He didn't make her breathless. He wasn't this elemental force like Matteo. A whirlwind she wanted to be swept away by.

Where had that thought come from?

'Are you ready, or do you still need more time?'

As Matteo walked towards her she closed her sketch pad. Something about him seeing what she did made her feel vulnerable. She drew pictures for children's books whereas he ran a global company worth…she didn't know how much, but a man who had a private jet and houses all over the world must be doing very well for himself.

'No, I'm ready.'

From the clothes Matteo had organised for her there was nothing she'd selected that looked at all beachy so her dress would have to do. She took off her glasses and left them on the drawing board before they headed out of the house, down a paved pathway towards the lake. Passing pots overflowing with a riot of flowers. Petunias. Geraniums. Bougainvillea. The place so unlike her cool green home. Everything here somehow…supercharged.

Hyper-real.

'Do you stay at this house often?'

She had so many questions. Even though you could search for him online, it really didn't tell her much about the man. All she knew was from that brief summer as children and her conversations with Mae. How well he'd done. How he and his family didn't get along. But she was sure there was so much more to him. She just didn't know why she wanted to know it all.

Matteo shrugged. 'Not really. Not anymore.'

He'd walked ahead a little, his long powerful stride making her scurry to catch up, though she couldn't really complain. This way she could get a glimpse of his broad shoulders, how well his shorts fitted, moulding to his body. Was it objectifying? She wasn't sure. Did he do the same to her? Even the thought he might made her cheeks heat.

'What made you stop?'

He slowed his steps so she could catch up. 'Circumstance. Business. I don't stay anywhere for long.'

Not having any real place to call home, no matter how beautiful the surroundings, seemed surreal to her. 'I can't imagine travelling around all the time.'

'I can't imagine not. You can make the world as large or as small as you want. I prefer mine large.'

'Is that like saying, "You need to get out more, Louisa"?'

He chuckled and she loved the sound of it. Warm, rolling with a twist of wickedness. The way it made her tingle, want to curl up her toes in her shoes. He turned to her, smiled. That smile was like a mouthful of hot chocolate on a winter's day. Rich, decadent. Addictive.

'I am.'

People had tried before, even Mae. So many not understanding why she was happy to live in Easton Hall. No one could comprehend her past, how a stable home was everything she'd ever wanted. How much she owed to Mae. The woman had given up years of her life to look after a broken teenager. It was the least Louisa could do, to give up some years of her life looking after Mae in return.

What drove Matteo to remain constantly on the move? There had to be something behind it. Wasn't it normal to seek a home, to have a retreat, a singular place to stay? Though she supposed he made retreats all over the world.

That was his business, what he did. Homes away from home for the rich and famous, when he didn't personally have one he called his own.

They rounded a corner following a manicured path through a small copse of trees, which then opened onto an expanse of grass with the magnificent lake beyond.

'Almost there,' Matteo said as he began to walk a little faster, almost as if he was excited. She picked up her pace to keep up with him. After a short distance the path led to a tiled terrace with a balustrade overlooking the lake. Stairs, down to the water.

'I'm sorry I couldn't give you sand. Pebbles will have to do.'

She followed him down the stairs and onto the pebbles of the private beach, uneven under her ballet flats. In a few spots along the bank there were artfully planted trees. Under one ancient tree sat an outdoor table, chairs.

The magnificent blue of Lake Como lay out in front of her. Mountains framing the scene. The late afternoon sun, warm on her body. A cool breeze caressing her skin. The magic of the scene seemed to unknot her. Her shoulders slowly dropping. Tension in her neck loosening. Matteo kicked off his shoes, walked to the water's edge and waded in to his calves, overlooking the view as if he ruled the whole lake. She followed to the water's edge and a shiver ran through her. How it seemed so dark and impenetrable.

'You coming in?' he asked.

She'd love to be like him, take off her shoes, throw away caution, but a little voice began whispering in her head.

'My mother would never have approved.'

Why did that woman still enter her consciousness, always holding her back whenever she wanted something for herself?

'Why not?' Matteo asked.

'Well, for one, germs. She'd say you never knew what lurked in unchlorinated water.'

He snorted. 'Every day is about risk. Your mother's not here now.'

No, she wasn't. Louisa walked to the water's edge. Took off her shoes, the creamy pebbles cool under her feet. Water lapping the edges just ahead. It all seemed so overwhelming, how fathomless all of this was. It was as if the world shifted under her feet and she was trying to find steady ground.

Then she looked over at Matteo. His patient smile. Somehow, everything seemed to solidify.

'Come on in,' he said. Could he see her struggle? Years of conditioning that was sometimes difficult to shake. Her dress brushed at her calves. It might get wet, though she supposed she could hold it up. There were so many decisions…

Matteo walked back towards her, the water sluicing around his legs till he was only ankle deep. 'I'm warning you, it's probably a bit cold given the lake's fed by the mountains. But you'll like it—'

'I don't know how to swim.'

The words simply blurted out of her. It seemed like such a huge failing. Another thing her mother had stopped her from doing.

'What if I'm not there when you're swimming, and you drown?'

Always so much fear. Louisa hadn't understood at

the time, but now she believed it had less to do with love and more to do with control. Her mother had never stopped to think that the greatest risk to Louisa's health was not knowing how to save herself. Or maybe she hadn't really cared.

Matteo frowned. 'You don't know...'

His voice was incredulous, drifting off as if he couldn't even finish the sentence.

'How to swim.' Her voice, in contrast, sounded firm, because she wasn't broken. Not many people knew how much she'd endured, what it had taken to survive. She just needed to convince herself of that strength, some days.

Sunlight glittered on the water's surface. It looked so inviting, if she could forget the fears that plagued her when faced with something new.

'The water's shallow here. There's no drop off. Take my hand.'

She hesitated. Matteo held out his arm, palm up. That gentle, encouraging smile still warming his face.

'I won't let you fall.'

She looked down at her feet, toes so close to the water. Took a deep breath. Hitched her dress into her underwear as something about Matteo's gaze darkened, melted. Then she reached out, his warm fingers clasped about her own as he gently guided her to him. At the first touch of the icy water on her feet she sucked in a breath, her heart skipping in her chest as he drew her close.

Not into his arms as she had been earlier in the day when they'd first arrived. In that moment when his body had felt so hard and solid. Initially she was just trying to be thankful till it morphed into something else. Something she refused to give voice to but would keep her up late in the dark of her own bedroom. Fuel for the drawings only she would ever see in that secret sketchbook. Her fantasies, where they'd always remain. How could there be a reality with him? She could never forget he was the enemy.

Yet why did she feel as if he was turning into something else?

Matteo squeezed her fingers. 'Not so bad?'

She shook her head. There was no bad in this moment. It was all good. Really good. Something bubbled up inside her, an unusual sensation. Joy. A sense of freedom. Like when she'd been a child and sent to Mae's. Even though her father was ill she'd used to play in the stream on the grounds of Easton Hall. Especially the summer Matteo came to stay too. She'd had no fears then, not really. At the time she hadn't understood her father was going to die. She was a child who wanted to forget that her dad was sick, and her mum wasn't emotionally available.

Matteo had seemed so brave then, that little bit older, a bit wilder. And after a while they'd played in the stream together. Explored secret corridors behind the walls of the house. Eaten a glut of berries from the kitchen garden till their hands and lips were stained and their bellies ached.

She could be like that child again. Full of wonder, wanting to explore. Louisa realised somewhere during her journey over the past twelve years she'd lost it, become stuck. She let go of his hand, slipped hers away from his warmth. That summer had created some of her best memories, ever. Together she and Matteo had always been up to something. Getting into all sorts of mischief...

Louisa gasped at a memory long buried.

'You made me kiss a frog.'

Was it her imagination, or had flags of red just flashed across Matteo's bronzed cheeks?

He placed his hand on his heart. 'Never.'

'No. You *did*. You found one and told me if I kissed it, it'd turn into a prince, marry me and I'd be able to have a tiara and a pony.'

'You're a children's book illustrator. Do you think you might be getting caught up in your own stories?'

There was a niggle of doubt now, that maybe she had it wrong. That unpleasant splinter that told her she wasn't enough. Not to keep her dad alive, not for her mum... Yet she looked over at Matteo and the corner of his mouth quirked in a sly grin. Like that recalcitrant frog prince she'd been trying and failing to draw just the way she wanted him.

She pointed at him, waggling her finger. 'You. You're fibbing.'

He chuckled again, and the sound of it, that unrestrained mirth, made her toes curl into the pebbles beneath her feet in the cold waters of the lake.

'It wasn't one of my finest moments. But to be fair, I didn't think you'd fall for it.'

She planted her hands on her hips. 'You knew I'd do it.'

'How could I? It was clearly made up.'

'I was six.' She kicked her foot at him, and some water splashed over his calves. 'I hero-worshipped you.'

She looked down at his shorts, not wet exactly, but

the fabric darkened where some fat droplets of water had hit the fabric.

'Hero-worshipped me?' Something about the tone of his voice deepened. Became rougher, a bit like the gravel on the drive into his villa.

'You know it, and you loved it. You pretended not to, but you liked the fact I listened to everything you said *and* believed it.'

She kicked her foot again, and another splash of water hit his legs.

His gaze narrowed, became more intense, but that wicked quirk of his lips remained. 'You're playing a dangerous game.'

Louisa cocked her head, 'And what game is that?'

'If you don't stop now, it's one where you're about to get very wet.'

'You wouldn't dare.'

He reached his hand into the water and flicked some at her. She kicked back at him, and this time water hit his shirt.

'Right.'

He began surging towards her so she grabbed her skirts higher and giggled, running up onto the stones of the beach as he followed. She tried to run faster but her dress was too long, and she wasn't really trying very hard anyhow. Her heart pounded as pebbles crunched behind her and she took off. Heart thump, thump thumping in her chest. Trying to make it to the stairs, laughing now because there was something about this that was such a thrill. Everything forgotten but the chase.

She suspected Matteo wasn't trying very hard either. It was more about the anticipation than the capture…

Till an arm snaked round her waist and she was pulled against a solid, muscular body.

She squealed and kicked her feet as he swung her into his arms and moved back to the water's edge, waded in, the sound of it rushing with each strong stride.

'Don't you dare!' she squealed.

'I told you.'

She squirmed some more but if he let her go now, she'd be in the water.

'I don't believe you will,' she huffed, looking up at him. His eyelashes so long. Gaze heated. Eyes sparkling with mischief and something far darker.

'Play with fire, get burned.'

'We're in water, that saying doesn't work.'

'You know what I mean. I told you I'd get you wet. I keep my promises.'

Something about this moment was loaded. His strong hold, her squirming against him. How she was so hot it was as if she'd go up in flames. How the thought of being dropped into ice-cold water right about now seemed almost welcoming.

He cocked his eyebrow. 'What'll it be? Are you going to behave?'

She'd always behaved, always done everything she'd been asked. If she did, she'd been told, she'd get better. All lies. Right now, she wanted to change her script. To do something unexpected for the first time in her life.

'Why do I want to misbehave, to be bad so…badly?'

It was freeing, this sensation. She threw her head back and laughed.

'We can be a little bad,' he murmured as he lowered his head, his lips skimming her throat. Her laughter stopped on a gasp, the sensation of it like an electric shock. His lips gentle, drifting over her skin. There was no laughter now, the only sound from her was half sigh, half moan. Her nipples prickling in her bra. Heat arrowing between her thighs. The need for him all-encompassing.

She wanted. As she'd never wanted anything or anyone before. It overwhelmed her, her whole body a mess of sensation.

Did he want her as much as she craved him?

His lips traced back towards her face, her jaw. Light brushes till she turned her head and their lips touched. Breaths intermingled. Slow, luxurious. Hypnotic. She became a captive of the sensation. Opening for him. His tongue slipped into her mouth, the barest of touches with her own.

Then the kiss slowed, stopped.

Matteo pulled back, looked deep into her eyes. Pupils blown wide, his own irises almost black.

'Before I drop you in the deep end, I need to teach you how to swim first. Slow, gentle steps.'

Could he see it on her face, the *need*? If self-combustion were a thing, she'd have gone up in his arms. Burned them both away to ash till they mingled and drifted out across the lake. He could be talking about swimming, she supposed, but she was sure this was something more.

What had just happened between them? How could she have let it?

Matteo walked out of the water, released her, letting her go slowly, and she slid down the full length of his body. So hard and uncompromising. She was almost disappointed that he hadn't carried out his threat, or promise, or whatever that all just was. The thoughts and sensations tangled through her in a mess of desire.

'I'd like that.' Her voice was breathless, as though she'd run a mile. Though his was probably a false promise. People had made those to her all the time, especially her mother.

'Take this medicine, it'll make you feel better.'

'This doctor will cure you.'

Any medicine only made her sicker, and no doctor could cure her because there'd never been anything wrong in the first place.

Those thoughts were like being plunged unceremoniously into the deep, dark waters of the lake. All the heat, all the want, simply…gone.

Matteo nodded and whatever had just happened between them passed.

'I—I should get back to work,' she said, her limbs limp like overcooked pasta. She wasn't sure her legs would carry her back to the house.

'I'll see you at dinner, then. It'll be around eight. I'll come and find you.'

'Thank you. Until then.'

She grabbed her shoes. Began walking back to the stairs, almost stumbling as she went, she was so unsteady. He didn't follow, just remained standing on the pebbled beach.

'I'd like to see what you do,' he called out from behind her, almost like an afterthought. 'Your drawings.'

Now it was her turn to nod.

Though she tended not to allow anyone to see her work until it was finished. As though if someone witnessed

what she was doing, the magic would suddenly be gone.
'Once I have something to show you.'

'I'll look forward to it.'

She wasn't sure why she found that so hard to believe.

CHAPTER SEVEN

HE'D MADE A serious error of judgement. It had been days since those moments at the lake where some kind of enchantment had overtaken him and he'd brushed his lips across Louisa's perfect, tempting throat as she laughed. Lost any sense in the moment. Took her perfect mouth with his own.

Why do I want...to be bad...so badly?

That same phrase could apply to him as well. From the moment his lips had touched her skin, he'd been a condemned man. Doomed to crave more of her. Her gasp, the breathy moan. The way she'd opened for him. Tongue tentatively touching his own. It was all he could think about. Whereas Louisa?

He wasn't sure. Fearing he'd frightened her. He knew passion and desire, and believed she'd been as affected as him. The colour high on her cheeks as she'd slid down his body. The way her breath had hitched. Nipples obvious points against the soft fabric of her dress. Except, now, it was as if she'd disappeared. Locking herself away with her artwork. Barely coming out for meals as if she'd been avoiding him. All he knew was that Louisa was keeping to herself. So absorbed, it was as if he didn't exist.

He needed to apologise for it, fix it somehow, even

though he wasn't sorry at all. His body craved more of her. His mind? Matteo shook his head, trying to get the persistent vision of her head thrown back in his arms, her laughter, from it. How he'd imagined her head thrown back, not in laughter, but in ecstasy...

He couldn't. Shouldn't.

Why?

That one word had run through his head like a broken record. They were both adults. Clearly attracted to each other.

Why, why, why?

He could add more words to that single one his brain locked onto, like some kind of chant. *Sheltered, innocent.* He'd lost his own innocence years ago. Life teaching him how cold and cruel it could be. Yet that afternoon on the lake when he'd shown Louisa her first beach, he'd simply *taken*. Thinking more clearly, as he was now, for someone who'd lived her life locked away it must have come as a shock. He should apologise. Her avoiding him, becoming fearful of the world, was not part of his plan.

Eyes on the prize, Matteo.

Louisa had her whole life, now in front of her. A world she needed to see. A right to reside she needed to relinquish. He wasn't going to get that by seduction, as tempting as she was.

Matteo made his way to the space he now called her workroom. Knocked gently. Opened the door when there was no answer because she might be avoiding him, but they *needed* to talk. Perhaps she was walking about the grounds. She seemed to love the gardens here. He'd catch flashes of her gleaming copper hair in fiery contrast to the trees and shrubbery, but when he went to find her, she'd be gone. Disappearing like a ghost.

It was beyond frustrating. As was the way she'd been so non-committal about him seeing her artwork. It wasn't as if she'd said no.

It was that she hadn't really said anything at all.

He walked to her drawing table, art supplies neatly put away. The sketchbooks that she drew in, stacked beside it. He looked at a few scraps of paper tacked to the table, almost like a mood board. Sketches of ink pen, a little frog in a crown. A frog with personality judging by the way that crown sat slightly askew. An almost… smirk on its wide froggy mouth. Her attention to detail, the frog's princely little outfit. A red fitted jacket that looked like velvet though how she'd achieved that with pen, ink and what appeared to be coloured pencil was beyond him. Little yellow-and-blue-striped bloomers. His spotted skin. It was extraordinary.

He smiled. Wanting to find out more about the story she illustrated. To his shame he'd not paid much attention, and this was such an integral part of who Louisa *was*. Committed to her work, clearly taking pride in it, worried about deadlines.

He glanced at the carefully stacked sketch pads.

'Her work's really something.'

The words of that contractor who'd packed away her things. He'd almost berated the man for looking but why should this artwork be hidden? Yet another temptation in his path, yet this wouldn't hurt anyone if he gave into it. A quick scan of her illustrations and he'd leave. Continue looking for her. Which one to choose? He grabbed the sketch pad at the top, one with a beige cover. Placed it on the tabletop and opened.

These drawings were different from the sketches tacked to her desk. No whimsy about them at all. Pages filled with dark ink and nightmare creatures hiding in the shadows with twisted faces and evil grins. Hands reaching out of the darkness.

Nightmares.

That night of the storm. The cry that had him out of bed. Had that been Louisa? A heat rose inside him, like anger. He wanted to know what had caused the fear and horror he saw on these pages. To *fix* it, somehow. Matteo kept turning more pages, and the pictures changed. Drawings of people now, or disembodied parts of them at least. Hands, feet, eyes. All in exquisite detail.

They somehow felt intimate. However, he didn't think they were from life. Still, the bitter spike of something like jealousy overcame him, because they were all of a man. Although there was a familiarity about the sketches. Matteo couldn't put his finger on it… He kept going, and then he saw it. A full drawing of the statue of David on one page. On the other, Louisa had drawn him, not as the statue, but as if he were a real person. They must be from pictures. She'd never travelled before. The brilliance of them, sketching marble then making that marble come to life in pencil, pen and ink.

He should stop. This book was obviously private, unlike the sketches for her work. Yet he couldn't. He was like a man possessed. Here was the woman she hid. What other secrets would he find? He wanted to know more of what made Louisa tick. He flicked over pages of detailed drawings, until the drawings changed again.

A sketch of a couple. If he'd thought that the pictures of David were somehow intimate, this *was* about intimacy. She'd inked so few lines on the page yet there was no hiding what this drawing was about. The pair, naked. You couldn't see their faces but there was no doubt what they were doing. He turned the page, another scene. A couple lying on a bed. Rumpled sheets. The man's hand lazily resting on the woman's stomach. This was like looking through a window, except into Louisa's soul. Then the detail drawings. Hands clutching sheets, backs arched. Fingers pressing into flesh. Bodies connected.

Heat roared over him, rushing low. The weight of his desire overcoming sensible thought. He couldn't stop turning page after page. They were magnificent, erotic. Couple after couple making love, kissing. Touching. Questing mouths and hands. Such a contrast to the innocence Louisa always portrayed to the world. He lost himself in her pictures, not thinking whether he should or shouldn't.

Not thinking much, other than about a need to see *more*. He fixed on the last picture, a naked couple entwined, wrapped together and also wrapped in what looked like…wind. With scattered leaves whirling about them as if they'd both been picked up into the air. The woman, hair long and wild, curling round them both in the maelstrom. The man. Dark hair, mouth at her throat…

Were they her fantasies? In a general continuum of the acts of lovemaking they were tame enough. But that they'd come from her at all, given for the best part of her life she'd been isolated… Here he'd spent time berating himself for kissing her, yet these pictures weren't soft sketches filled with innocent love and romance. They scorched the pages with yearning and passion. A need he knew exactly how to fulfil…

'What are you doing?'

He hadn't heard the door open. Matteo snapped the sketchbook shut. A fresh heat burned through him but this wasn't desire, it was something like shame.

Louisa looked to the sketchbook under his fingers and stormed up to him, eyes narrowed, lips thin in anger. She reached out, hand trembling. Snatched the book from the desk's surface, holding it to her chest.

'You had no right. That's private.' Her voice was so quiet. As if he'd somehow forced his way into her life and exposed her deepest secrets. Her face flushed red. Her pale skin hiding nothing. He liked the way she blushed, but this time it wasn't something sweet and innocent. The way her mouth dropped, it was as if she were humiliated.

'I know.'

The taint of guilt slicked over him then. He'd embarrassed her by invading her space, her privacy. It had been the wrong thing to do and he was sorry, in some ways. In others, he wasn't sorry at all. Because he'd learned something about Louisa today.

That she desired.

'They're things you shouldn't have looked at. Things I never—'

'I'm sorry, Lu— Louisa.'

She whipped round, her hair swirling like the woman in the last picture, long, loose. Glorious. Like this, in her fury, it was as if she were on fire.

'Oh, really? Then why were you in here?'

He held his hands out, placating. 'I was looking for you. I didn't know where you were, and I haven't seen you much over the past few days. I thought you were avoiding me.'

'I was *working*. Something I thought you might understand.'

'I do.' Or at least, he did now. He'd not really thought much about her work before. When she'd first worried about missing her deadline and needing her things he'd dismissed her, told her she should take a break. To have fun. Now… 'You're exceptionally talented.'

Her skin flared an even brighter red. Louisa chewed on her lower lip. Clutching the sketch pad to her chest. Her fingers blanched white around the edges.

'You know what I think?' he went on. 'I think you're feeling ashamed right now of what I've seen, and you shouldn't.'

'How do you know *anything* about what I'm feeling?'

'Because I'm human. Those pictures are all about humanity. Passion. It isn't something to be ashamed of, or to hide. It's normal, and I won't judge you for it.'

It was as if she almost folded in on herself. Shoulders drooping. Hair covering her face. 'You're lying.'

'Why would I lie?'

He wanted her to face him, to be proud of what he'd seen. Instead, she snorted, turned her back to him. Walked to the French doors overlooking the lake and stared outside.

'People lie all the time, Matteo. They say one thing, mean another. Think only about themselves, not caring who they hurt in the process.'

His gut clenched, hard and angry. He wanted to ask who had hurt her. Who'd put that haunted look on her face. Who'd made her draw, not those pictures of lovemaking and ecstasy, but the darker ones. The ones that looked like, not what she craved, but what she feared. Yet he was also angry at himself. How wounded she appeared, all because of his curiosity, when he should have known better.

People were entitled to their secrets. She could keep hers. All he'd been looking for was a way in, and he'd found it. Anything to show her that living in a huge old home in the country with only staff for company was a waste. That she was a woman of passion and desire. Someone who clearly wanted more, and the world was there for her taking.

He needed to repair what he'd done here. She wanted truth, and he wanted trust. The only way he could achieve either was to give a tiny bit of himself. Not one that would crack him open *too* wide, but enough for Louisa to know that he was telling the truth.

Matteo shook his head, began to prise open the vault to the memories he preferred to keep hidden. Part of him rebelled at the disclosure, because truths could cause the most painful of wounds if twisted against you. But this was Louisa. *Lulu.* As harmless as a kitten.

'I know what it's like to be lied to,' he said, 'and I promised myself I'd never do that to another person. Even if the truth hurt.'

Louisa held on to her sketchbook as if it were a kind of life preserver. The only thing keeping her afloat. The one she'd especially wanted nobody to see. It contained her darkest nightmares, where the fear overcame her. Waking her in the night. Compelling her to draw because if she captured them on paper, they might stop tormenting her. Then those other dreams, her fantasies. The ones that taunted her in another way. She'd captured them to make them real, because she'd never wanted a relationship but, sometimes, she *wanted*. In the end she'd learned that dreams couldn't hurt you. Not like people.

People were all risk. Little reward.

Though the way she'd seen Matteo when she'd stood at the door, paralysed. The intensity on his face as he looked at her most private sketchbook. The unalloyed fascination as his hands touched the pages gently, almost reverently.

Before the shock and anger overtook her, she'd imagined those fingers touching her.

That last drawing, two people caught in a whirlwind. She'd felt like that down at the lake, in his arms. When his lips slipped over her skin. Their kiss, which rocked the very core of her. It was like discovering a part of herself that had been missing for so long. Here, in this glorious sunshine, far from everywhere familiar, the fears that plagued her nights had begun leaching away. Turning into something more heated, insistent like a ceaselessly beating drum.

Need.

He'd been right, she had been avoiding him. Her work being a convenient excuse. But she couldn't think about that right now, not with the man those recent desires had begun tangling round standing right in front of her. A man who claimed he knew how much untruths hurt. If they talked about him, he wouldn't talk about her and what he'd seen.

'Who lied to you?'

He turned away, walking to the glass doors overlooking the lake, hands in his pockets. As if he was trying to distance himself from some memory. Nothing about him was open right now. He'd closed himself off from her.

'When I was six, an older cousin told me I wasn't a real Bainbridge. That I was adopted and I'd never be one of them. I was a fake, a phony. Until then, I'd had no idea.'

Her stomach dropped. She couldn't imagine what that would have been like. How could anyone say that to a child? Though she understood this family. They were only after perfection, not failure. Blood and legacy were the only things important to any of them.

'Matteo, I'm—'

He cut off her words of sympathy with the slice of his hand through the air. Okay, so he didn't want to talk about it. That she understood all too well. The sympathetic looks from the police after her mother had finally been found out. The empathy from her psychologist. In the end she was sick of it all. Of being thought of as unwell for so many years, then being thought of as somehow broken. When all she'd wanted was for things to go back to how they were before her father died. When she was a normal child with her whole life ahead of her.

'It was a gift,' he said, yet his voice sounded choked. 'I finally realised why my parents didn't treat me the same as Felicity. Sent me away when she got sick. It made sense. I wasn't theirs.'

She shook her head. 'No, that can't be right.'

'It can. What other explanation is there?'

'Your parents had adopted you. They *wanted* you.'

He turned. Mouth a thin, brutal line.

'They wanted what every Bainbridge wants. An heir. Someone to carry on the family wealth, the family name if they're lucky enough to have a boy. Don't worry, I've reconciled myself to the realisation.'

Yet everything about him now seemed so hard and tense. As if one wrong move and he'd crack and break into a million pieces.

'Have you?'

'It is what it is. I can't change it. They got their true heir in the end.'

'Are you sure about that? What about Felicity?'

'What about her?'

Louisa had been surprised to see Felicity at Mae's funeral. It had been clear she was a Bainbridge, the pale skin and hair a giveaway, yet Louisa had never met her before. Then she'd introduced herself, whilst seeming to search the small crowd of mourners as if looking for something, or someone...

'I get the idea you don't see her much. Have you asked her whether it's what she wanted? Whether she thinks of herself as the sole heir?'

He shook his head. 'Of course not. I don't see her because she's working as a nanny and travels a lot. Both of us are busy.'

He reached almost reflexively into his pocket, pulled out his phone. Seemed to think better of it, shoved it back as if it might burn him. Louisa knew all about avoidance of the things that hurt you the most. Sometimes the greatest kindness was to let someone hide.

Hadn't she been hiding long enough?

'Did you want to see some of my illustrations?'

Matteo's eyes widened at the sudden change of subject. 'I'd love to see what you want to show me.'

Words loaded, replete with meaning. Was there an answer?

Everything.

No. Where did that come from?

She didn't know. These thoughts, they intruded when she was around him. Insistent things that whispered she was entitled to whatever reward Matteo could provide to her. She'd waited long enough.

'I don't really show people my work before it's finished.' She grabbed a sketchbook and placed it on her table. Sure, she'd struggled with the pictures, and these were the sorts of drawing she'd generally file in a cabinet when done. Putting the characters who'd invaded her brain to bed. When she gave her drawings over for the last time, it was as if she set her characters free. And set herself free as well…till the next project held her captive.

'Why?'

How to explain something that made little sense, even to her? 'It's like when I share my illustrations, they stop being mine and become someone else's. Like the other person takes some of the magic away.'

He hesitated then, his hand halting over the page.

'I don't want to ruin the magic for you. I know how important your work is.'

Something inside her warmed. He understood part of what this meant to her. Her mother had always disparaged her 'doodling'. In spite of the woman, she'd built a career on it but still occasionally heard that critical voice, telling her what she was doing had no value.

'It's okay,' she said.

'I feel privileged.' Matteo's voice carried a weight, as though he meant it. 'What book are you illustrating?'

'A reimagining of *The Frog Prince*.'

'Always children's stories?'

She nodded. 'I like them, the innocence of it. And I love the idea that something I'm doing is giving children joy.'

The only thing that had given her much happiness as a child was reading. In those illustrated children's books she'd found an escape. Some days, after her father had died, when she was in and out of hospital, books and the fantasy world she could immerse herself in were all that had kept her going. It had been something her mother couldn't steal from her.

She wanted to give that escape to other children as well.

'Have you ever thought of writing your own?'

Louisa stilled. There were other sketchbooks. The stories she'd written and drawn for Mae. About two children and their stupendous summer adventures, which had made Mae laugh. But they were more personal, private things. Created because she'd wanted to make a woman she loved remember happier times. Some of the happiest times of Louisa's own life.

Still, she shook her head. 'It's not for me. Let the author take the accolades. I'm not really into the idea of book signings and publicity.'

Matteo frowned, skewered her with his hot brown gaze that saw too much, even though he didn't say anything in response.

She opened the first page of her sketchbook and slid it over to him.

'Here are some working drawings, the ones I did when I was a bit stuck.'

They stood side by side. The man somehow radiated heat. The warmth from his body slid through her. His presence was palpable as a touch, like a finger gently stroked down her spine. Goosebumps skittered across her skin.

How could the proximity of a person do this to her? This sparkling sensation that lit up every nerve of her body. Made her catch her breath whenever he was close.

Made her want him closer...

Matteo chuckled, dragging her away from those tempting thoughts. He'd turned to the page of the frog she'd sketched the day he'd first rung the doorbell at Easton Hall.

'He looks like a frog with attitude.'

'He was giving me trouble. He always has.'

'Have you wrestled him into submission now?'

She laughed. 'That's not really the way it works for me. They have a mind of their own. Sometimes they don't want to be drawn the way you want to draw them. Hence these sketches. Trying to convince him to do what I wanted.'

'That sounds—'

'Odd. I get it.'

No one truly understood. They nodded with a fixed smile on their face when she tried to tell them.

'No, it sounds fascinating. Like to get the perfect drawing you have to understand the characters, and for that, they become real. That takes some imagination, Lulu. I don't know how you do it.'

She stilled at his slip. The use of her nickname. Yet

he didn't seem to have noticed. Perhaps she was reading too many things into it. Her imagination had always been the safest place to reside, after all. It was easy. Real life, that was the hard thing. She still struggled with it.

'I don't know how you run a multimillion-dollar business.'

'Billion-dollar.' The corner of his perfect lips quirked. 'Add a few more zeros.'

She laughed and smacked him in the arm. 'Sorry, Mr Businessman, for underestimating the number of zeros your business has.'

'My business is easy. It's about understanding what people want and giving it to them.'

Could he see what she wanted? Could he imagine it at all? A shiver ran through her. She repeatedly imagined seeing his body now, having felt it under his clothes. Obsessed about looking at every part of him. Even though some days she thought he could peer right inside her soul, he wasn't a mind reader. Except, he'd seen those intimate drawings. They were her imaginings too. It wouldn't take much to connect that those desires now involved him.

Which was another of the reasons she'd hid. Wanting him; when he was the man who sought to take everything away from her. Though he hadn't mentioned anything over recent days. Maybe he didn't need to add Easton Hall to his empire after all?

'I call what you do impossible,' she said.

'I call your illustrations impossible. But here we are, proving we're both making the impossible happen.'

He reverently turned a few more pages. The way he touched the paper again. Gently. With long, strong-looking fingers topped by perfect square nails. Drifting over the paper, almost as though he wanted to feel the drawings on the page.

'Extraordinary,' he murmured. The word was so quiet, it was almost like an exhale. There was something about his reverence that slid through her with pleasure. Winding its way on a seductive journey through her blood, heating her from the inside out.

'Thank you. The work seems to have become a bit easier here, since I've settled in. Something about the sunshine. It's making everything brighter.'

He looked up at her, slowly, almost assessing. As if he'd come to himself and remembered something long forgotten. 'I should let you get back to it, then. So you can finish. When you're done, I'd like to take you out to dinner.'

'Oh.'

Louisa didn't know what to say. She'd never been invited out to dinner by anyone before. A tiny kind of thrill skittered round her belly. She wasn't sure if it was based on excitement or on fear.

'There's a little *trattoria* close by,' he said. 'It's hidden away, used more by locals than by tourists, so it won't be too crowded. How long do you think you might be? I thought we could celebrate meeting your deadline.'

'Maybe a day or two?'

He smiled. 'It's a date.'

She nodded as he walked from the room. A date? That was simply an expression. It meant nothing. Though Louisa didn't know why she simultaneously wished it were true.

And hoped it wasn't.

CHAPTER EIGHT

MATTEO STOOD, WAITING. Glass of Scotch in hand. His phone buzzed an alert, which he checked. The car would be here soon to take them to his favourite little restaurant in town, tucked away in a cobbled alley. He'd asked the owner to set up a table for a celebration. Initially they'd thought it represented an engagement until he'd disabused them. He'd told them it was a special night nonetheless, and the owner seemed somehow pleased, promising a table in a quiet corner.

His plans seemed to be working. Louisa's talk of how the sunshine helped her pictures. He'd known getting her away from the UK would work, though the reasons seemed a little hazy right now. The raging desire for revenge not quite as sharp. He mused why that might be. Working seven days a week for months might be the cause. Likely he'd needed a break too. To simply stop and enjoy the sunshine himself…

Matteo downed the last, short sip in his glass, settling the strange sensation in his gut that had overcome him. Almost like anticipation, but that couldn't be right. He checked his watch. Almost time to go. This was a simple meal, nothing more. Another step in showing Louisa that there was more to life than living in the rainy old

English countryside. She could chase the sunshine all round the world, if she wanted, he just needed to make her feel as if it were her idea.

'I'm ready now.'

Louisa. It was as though his imagination had conjured her. He turned, ready to let her know the car was about to arrive, except his voice was stolen. Simply dying in his throat.

She was unlike he'd ever seen her before. Dressed not like someone who'd stepped out of the past, but like a woman who slammed him straight into his future. A vision in green. The dress still long, soft and flowing, but cinched at the waist with a golden chain. The fabric vibrant and silky, lovingly caressing her curves. The front dipped into a tantalising vee between her breasts. Round her bare shoulders she wore a sheer wrap in the same colour as the dress, yet threaded through with gold like the chain, so it shimmered under the lights. Her hair tumbled round her shoulders and down her back in gleaming copper waves.

He froze, struck silent. As if this was a moment in time he wanted to stay captured in for ever. Like a scene from a movie, the type written about in books. A realisation that this woman was nothing like she seemed.

The blood in his veins rushed low as if he were some teenager, and he willed his body under control. Why was he so surprised? She was a stunning woman. He'd known that. Yet something about tonight seemed to have woven her in a kind of magic.

She gave a tremulous smile and tightened the wrap round herself. Was she still insecure about how she looked? In that moment, Matteo wanted to hurt whoever had ever made her doubt herself, her appearance. Her style.

'You look exquisite.'

His voice ground out all rough and dark, as if he'd just found it after years of silence. Her eyes widened, cheeks flushed a glorious pink. If he had buttons to push, she was activating every single one with her soft, alluring innocence. Completely unaware of how she affected him.

'Thank you.'

Her own voice sounded breathless. As if she couldn't believe what he was saying now. What he'd told her before.

You are beautiful. That's a fact and not open for discussion.

'I—I wasn't sure about the dress, but it was a celebration so...'

'It's magnificent on you.' That earned another flush of pleasure. He wanted more. To capture every one all for himself.

'And I'm surprised. It's not like what you usually wear.'

'Sylvana suggested it. For fun, to try out something different. She said the green would look lovely with my hair...or something.'

Yet another thing she'd been prepared to try that was new. What he'd been hoping for. Soon, she'd want to explore the world without him. Yet why did that thought give him the sense of a deadline? One he never wanted to meet.

'You look *beyond* lovely. You always do. But tonight, you could be a siren, luring a man to his doom.'

'Oh, I'm not sure about that.'

'Trust me. I'm a man.'

She gave him a small smile that was imbued with a shy kind of pleasure. 'And I'm luring you to your doom?'

'Right now, I'm hungry. Dinner first, doom later.'

Louisa threw back her head and laughed, the sound lighting up the room like a firework. He could listen to that unrestrained sound of pure joy, every day. His phone buzzed another alert and he pulled it from his pocket.

'Car's here.'

'I'm a little bit excited about this. I've never been to a restaurant before,' she said, almost like a throwaway line as they headed for the front door and he locked up.

Never been to a restaurant? It seemed inconceivable and yet there was no doubt in his mind she told the truth. It underscored once more how sheltered she was. How little he understood of her, or her life.

A driver held the car door open for them and Matteo helped Louisa in. Her hand soft and warm in his. She lifted her dress and he glimpsed a hint of golden shoes as she slid into the seat. Her slender ankles.

What was happening to him? When did the hint of cleavage and the sight of shapely ankles ever attract him before?

He couldn't say. But it seemed that they did now. He wanted to wrap his hands around her ankles as he eased her legs apart. Kiss up and up till his mouth reached the heart of her. Make her scream his name. Recollections of those drawings of hers flooded back. A man's head buried between a woman's thighs. Hand gripping his hair, holding him tight. Holding him in place. That was the meal he craved right now...

Matteo took a deep, steadying breath. Fantasies were

fine. It was the reality that could come back to bite you
and that was a sobering thought. She looked up at him
in anticipation, probably wondering why he was standing there. What would she do if she could delve inside
his head, read his imaginings? Run to him, or away?
He'd never know. Matteo hopped into the car next to
her. After a blissfully short drive achingly aware of her
presence next to him, they pulled up at a street at the
bottom of a hill.

'Are we here already? We could have walked!'

'We can walk back after the meal, if you like.'

He could imagine that. The moonlight over the lake.
Strolling back to the villa, hand in hand…

Where had that absurd thought come from? He'd never
once held hands with a woman.

Matteo shrugged it off as he hopped out of the car and
tipped the driver. Leading Louisa up a narrow street to a
red door in a centuries-old wall. Just a small sign with the
words Trattoria Galante announcing what lay behind. He
pushed it open and they walked through a softly lit hall.

'Signor Bainbridge!' The ebullient owner welcomed
him almost like a prodigal son returned. 'I have a special table for you both.'

They were led through premises bustling with locals,
with its old stone walls and tables with checked cloths, towards the rear. Louisa seemed a little wide eyed, almost
overwhelmed. He settled his hand on her back. Gently
guiding her through. Trying not to forget how new this
was for her. The bile rose to his throat. Anger at Mae,
for taking in a child who she seemed to have kept hidden
away rather than showing her the world. Not ever having
been to the beach. Never having eaten in a restaurant.

Why?

Mae had done all of those things before her husband had died. She must have known what a young woman needed out of life, and yet she'd kept Louisa there like some hermit. It made no sense.

He flexed his fingers on the small of her spine. He'd started now, and he'd complete the job. She wouldn't want to go back to Easton Hall after he'd finished with her. He could take her to all his properties. His boutique hotel in Paris, his resort in the Maldives. His island in Australia. There were any number of places and he'd show them all to her...

Except that wasn't his job. His job was to set her free and watch her fly. Yet the ideas took hold and wouldn't let go. How he'd love to see her bury her toes in pristine white sand for the first time. Step into the turquoise waters of a tropical beach. To watch her relish the food at each of the finest restaurants he knew. He could show her the world, yet somehow, he knew...

That was the most dangerous fantasy of them all.

They sat alone in a small courtyard. Above them strings of lights wound through a vine-covered pergola glimmered like fireflies. Candles flickered on the table, lending everything a soft glow. It looked as if she'd been dropped into some kind of wonderland. If she'd allowed herself to dream of the perfect date, then this would have come close.

Of course, dreams couldn't hurt you. Not like people. People were all risk. Little reward.

Anyhow, she'd never have a date because relationships weren't in her repertoire. What was the point of a relationship if you didn't want love? That hadn't ever been something she'd searched for, not romantic love at least. Love didn't mean happiness to her. Her mother had said she'd loved her and done terrible things. Love meant loss, obsession. Something unhealthy.

There was nothing healthy about it.

That didn't mean she couldn't enjoy tonight, though she wouldn't let her imagination run away from her. Matteo was simply being kind again. He'd used the word 'date' as a figure of speech, that was all. Yet it was as though he'd stolen a little piece of her heart when he'd brought her here to this romantic setting. The tableware gleaming. A pristine, starched white tablecloth. A little vase of geraniums adding a vibrant splash of colour in all the green.

She pulled her reading glasses from her small clutch, put them on and looked down at the menu, but it was in Italian. Her stomach grumbled.

Matteo chuckled. 'Hungry?'

He was so devastatingly handsome. He'd taken off his jacket, now sitting across from her in a white shirt that accentuated the golden colour of his skin. His eyes flickering chocolate in the candlelight.

'I don't understand anything on the menu.'

'There's no risk. Everything here's good but I can order if you like. Surprise you.'

Matteo picked up the menu himself, held it in his long, strong fingers. How they'd touched her as he'd guided her through to their table, sending a shiver of pleasure up her spine. How she wanted him to touch her like that again…

He smiled and a flicker of heat ignited deep inside her, glowing like the candles on the tabletop.

'Since this is a celebration, how about something that sparkles? Have you ever had champagne?'

The heat rose to her face. Embarrassment. What must he think of her, especially given her admission she'd never been to a restaurant before? The man was so…urbane. He probably drank champagne all the time.

'I wasn't totally sheltered. Mae opened a bottle on my sixteenth birthday. Dom Perignon, I believe.'

He raised an eyebrow. 'How forward-thinking of her.'

'In many ways, she was.'

A deep, unrelenting ache stabbed in her chest. She rubbed at it. Louisa missed Mae terribly. The love she'd shown Louisa. The care and patience. Allowing her to be herself, to find her way in her own time. Even though in later years Louisa seemed to have become somewhat… stuck.

No, not stuck. Settled. And there was nothing wrong with that.

'Did you enjoy it, the champagne?' Matteo asked.

'I remember it was fizzy and I thought it tasted sour, so not really. I only had a few sips.'

Matteo chuckled and the sound rippled right through her in waves of something like pleasure. 'Do you want to try again?'

Louisa slipped off her now unnecessary glasses and tucked them into her bag again, giving herself some time to answer. She could say no, but wasn't tonight all about trying something new? Different clothes, different food. Living, when everyone else she'd loved was dead.

'Why not?'

One of the waitstaff approached as if summoned tele-

pathically. Matteo ordered in Italian, barely even looking at the menu.

'So, what are we having for dinner?' she asked.

'It's a surprise.'

An uncomfortable sensation skittered through her
belly. Something almost like nerves. She always enjoyed
certainty. Her life at Mae's had been ruled by it. Though
nothing over the past weeks had been certain, and she'd
managed to survive it, so far.

'Don't you enjoy surprises?'

Matteo seemed to be able to pick up her emotions.
Sense what she needed. She didn't know how he managed it, but she didn't want to ruin tonight with her insecurities. Louisa shook her head.

'It's perfect. Thank you.'

'Finishing your illustrations is an achievement you
should be proud of. It's worth celebrating.'

'Do you celebrate your achievements?'

A slight frown creased his brow. 'Not really.'

'I guess you have so many. If you celebrated each one,
all that champagne. Would you ever be sober?'

His eyes widened for a moment, then he threw his
head back and laughed. She loved the sound. Deep,
throaty. The smile meeting his eyes, which crinkled at
the corners in amusement.

'There have been failures along the way. Don't think
I'm perfect.'

In so many ways, to her, he was. The hard, honed
businessman melting away. For the briefest of flashes,
he became Matty again. The young boy she'd remembered seeming to return, for rare moments at least.

She'd take those where she could grasp them, no matter how fleeting.

The waiter arrived once more with a bottle, which he opened with a slow hiss and pop. Poured. Matteo took his glass. Raised it to her.

'I hope you enjoy this a little better than your last attempt,' he said. 'To you, Louisa. Congratulations on finishing your illustrations on time.'

'I always finish them on time.' But the toast shouldn't be to her. It should be to someone else. Someone she felt was in so many ways forgotten in this story. She raised her own glass.

'To me,' she said, with tears in her eyes, 'and to Mae.'

He murmured in acknowledgement and their glasses clinked together. She took a sip of hers. The drink burst across her tongue, somewhat tart and refreshing. She swallowed, trying to look a bit sophisticated, but the bubbles tickled her nose and she coughed.

'You okay?' he asked.

'It's quite lovely.' And dangerous. It fizzed inside her the same way as her insides did when she looked at him. The way he made her feel alive. 'I think it's a drink that might get people into trouble.'

'I'm all for trouble.' He raised his glass again. 'Here's to that as well.'

It was her turn to laugh, but memories of Mae brought back memories of Easton Hall. As much as Lake Como and Matteo's villa were beautiful, Easton Hall was *home*. A home she wanted to go back to.

'What did the engineer say about the house?' she asked. Matteo's face blanked smooth as a pond on a windless day. He took a long sip of his champagne.

'He's assessed the structure. Insurance is next.'

Which didn't answer the most important question. 'When can I go back?'

'Easton Hall requires repairs and rewiring after the storm damage.'

'That might be the case, but it's my home.'

His eyes narrowed. His focus merciless, like a glaring spotlight in the dark. 'Where you locked yourself away.'

'No, I didn't.' It was as if a solid weight pressed on her chest, making it difficult to breathe. The place wasn't her prison. She'd made a life there, taking tourists on tours through the house. There wasn't a day she hadn't felt safe, secure. 'You don't understand.'

He sat back, eyebrow raised. 'Enlighten me.'

How could she share the terrible things her mother had done? So few people knew. Mae. Some doctors. The police. It had all been well hidden in the end. For the best, everyone said when her mother died. She didn't know where to even start, so she took another sip of champagne. Breathing through the relentless pressure bearing down on her. Before she was forced to say anything more, a waiter arrived with some food. A plate filled with pillowy-looking balls in a creamy sauce. The memories of her past faded with the scent of cheesy deliciousness.

She didn't want to look up and face Matteo's relentless gaze, so she ate. The flavour burst across her tongue in its richness. She moaned.

'Oh. My. Goodness. What is this?'

Matteo's fork was partway to his mouth. His eyelids hooded.

'It's a local speciality. Gnocchi with Taleggio cheese. Have you never had gnocchi before?'

She took another forkful and it was as if a world of flavour had opened up to her.

'No.'

Mrs Fancutt was a traditional cook, but her food was beautiful. Not quite like this, but it hadn't mattered to a half-starved child what she ate, so long as no one tried to stop her.

'Didn't you ever wish—?'

'I was happy for a home. That might be difficult for you to fathom.'

Matteo placed down his fork. 'I'm trying to understand.'

'There's nothing much to understand. I'm a simple person. A creature of habit. I like things the way I like things.'

'They keep you feeling safe,' he said.

Louisa stilled. It was the first time someone had voiced how she'd felt.

'Yes.'

'And stable?'

She nodded. How did he know?

'Because you lost your father and your mother and the world ceased to be a safe and stable place.'

'Yes.'

It was such a simple and painful summation of her life, even if lacking some important context.

'I understand.'

'Do you. Do you *really*?' How could anyone? But Louisa wanted him to. She *craved* it.

'When my cousin told me I wasn't a true Bainbridge and I confronted my parents, they said nothing would change. Then Felicity was born, was diagnosed with leukaemia.'

Matteo drained his glass. The waiter came and refilled it. Topped up hers.

'I was a little boy who was afraid he'd lose his sister,' he said, not quite looking at her. 'My parents didn't care. They sent me to boarding school, where I stayed. Forgotten. Everything I'd come to believe, that I should have parents who cared about me, a stable family—that ended. And I swore when I got older that I'd never be in that position again. So, I understand, Louisa. I understand all too well.'

She reached out to place her hand over his. Stopped. Matteo's face had hardened, the anger palpable in the air. She knew what it was like to be surrounded by sympathy when you didn't want it. When you wanted to forget, to move on. The problem was, you followed yourself wherever you went.

'That's what drove you,' she said.

'I created a life. I created a business. All *despite* my family.'

He'd been so shut off from her, and yet it was as if he'd opened a door to himself, no matter what it must cost him. What would it be like to share the burden of what had happened to her? Sure, she'd spoken to a psychologist in those early days. A person who was professional and at arm's length. But the only other person close to her who had known what had happened was Mae, and she was gone.

In that moment, Louisa had never felt so alone in the world. With no one to speak to when dark thoughts and nightmares had threatened to crush her. No friends, no family. She was orphaned in all respects. Yet Matteo was here. He seemed to want to listen.

And perhaps if he knew what had happened to her, he'd understand why Easton Hall was her safe place, one she never wanted to leave.

Matteo knew he was almost glaring at Louisa, daring her to say anything about what had happened to him. Yet she sat there in empathetic silence. When she'd reached out her hand to touch him, he'd craved her softness even though he didn't need it. He'd spent his life not needing others, because people let you down. He had himself, and that was enough.

Yet the disappointment when she pulled her hand away. He took a slow breath. No. He wasn't looking for sympathy. He'd been trying to understand, because if he was going to get Louisa to leave Easton Hall then she needed to trust him. To feel a connection.

It had all been calculated until the words had simply... left him. Things he'd spoken to no one about. Not even his own sister. How could he gripe about those old wounds to her when Felicity had almost died? So he'd cursed his family to hell instead. Yet why had the words felt so good leaving him? Like ridding himself of some kind of poison. All he knew was that he'd told her more than he'd planned, things that he tended to keep to himself, because if she understood him, perhaps she'd let him understand her.

He was sure there were things that she desired. She was just hesitant to reach out and take them. Well, he feared nothing.

'It seems we've both done things *despite* our families,' she said.

He nodded. 'My family cast me aside. Your parents passed away. It must have been hard, losing them so young.'

The waiter came and cleared their plates. Placed another exquisite dish on the table. A traditional fish speciality. He hoped Louisa enjoyed fish. Her first mouthful of the gnocchi seemed to have transported her in some kind of orgasmic bliss. He'd become instantly hard, realising that everything was new to her.

What he could introduce her to. All kinds of new experiences. How would she react? Those intimate sketches exposed her fantasies. He could show her reality. A heat began to stoke deep inside at the possibilities. Would she look at him with the same pleasure as she had eating a new food? How would she look being touched intimately for the first time...?

No. Once again he needed to remind his body that his job wasn't to seduce her. It was to convince her to leave Easton Hall. Yet wasn't that a seduction of sorts? He'd simply have to strike the right balance.

One that retained his sanity in the process.

'It was hard losing my father.' Louisa toyed with her fork, turning it as if staring at the candlelight reflected from the silver. Almost as if she was avoiding something. He guessed this would be a difficult conversation for her. At least she'd loved her parents. Had something to lose. His parents were still alive, and he'd lost them all the same.

Or perhaps, he'd never really had them at all.

He tried some of the fish, which was superb as always. Letting the silence stretch. It wasn't a comfortable one, but he knew that when people tried to fill it, they often made important disclosures. Louisa wasn't just a closed book, it was as if she were one written in a foreign language that he needed an interpreter to decipher.

'My mother…'

Here it was. The key, he was sure.

'She was arrested before she died.'

Everything in him stilled. Mae had never said anything to him about this, only that Louisa's story was a tragic one and hers to tell. He'd assumed that the tragedy was the death of both parents.

Clearly not.

Now he saw the space she'd left in the conversation as one for him to fill. As if what she had to say was too big and terrible to say without prompting. She dragged her bottom lip through her teeth, the evening taking on a terrible weight.

'Why was your mother arrested?' he asked.

Her knife and fork hovered above the plate. 'My mother…she…'

Louisa looked up at him, her eyes tight. Her knuckles whitening as she held her cutlery in a tight grip. His heart rate kicked up as he waited. She was opening herself up to him, but he wasn't sure what he'd find when she did.

Louisa's chest rose and fell as if she was taking a steadying breath.

'My mother was arrested because she used to hurt me.'

CHAPTER NINE

THE WORDS HAD been trapped, but Matteo's question had seemed to be the key to her voice, and they'd come out all in a rush. Maybe he hadn't heard. He simply sat there, staring at her. Mouth opening slightly as if wanting to speak. Closing. Then he put down his cutlery, knife and fork crossed on his plate.

'When you say "hurt"…'

The psychologist had known when Louisa had walked into their office what had happened. She'd received a referral, Louisa's records. Mae had known too. The only person she had ever really had to tell fresh was the police officer who took her statement.

She had never told another soul who hadn't known or suspected something of what had gone on first. Now it was as if she couldn't stop.

'My mother used to pretend that I was sick. When doctors didn't believe I was unwell, she'd *make* me sick. I spent time in hospital getting tests, having procedures, to find out what was wrong with me. There was nothing. For a while she convinced me that I wasn't well, and that if I didn't get treatment, I might die like my father had. Munchausen by Proxy, some people called it. Others called it Factitious Disorder Imposed on Another, which I always thought was a mouthful.'

Matteo reached out, took her hand in his. Squeezed her fingers.

Take my hand, Louisa.

Somehow, his touch made her feel braver.

'My God, I had no idea.'

'Nobody did.'

He shook his head. His thumb gently rubbing back and forth across her skin. Somehow settling her racing heartbeat, grounding her as memories of that time came flooding back.

'When did it start?'

'After my father died.'

'That's when you were only six. Just after…'

After she'd left Mae's for that last time. Her mother wouldn't let her go back, no matter how many times she'd asked to or Mae had invited her. Her mother probably knew Mae would see through the lies.

'Yes, just after that summer.'

'How did the doctors not see?'

That was a question she'd asked herself numerous times over the years since. Or the other, which he was kind enough not to voice.

Why didn't you say anything?

'My mother was clever. Doctors knew she was grieving. I believe they simply couldn't comprehend her being the one to make me ill, given my father had died. She told me that she was trying to make me better so that I didn't die like he did. That was an easy way to control a child because I was terrified. It was easy to make me look sick too. She started cutting back my food. Said I had intolerances. Fed me Dad's medications. I was always so thin and tired. Cutting my hair…'

Matteo made a wounded kind of noise, like coming deep from his soul. Clenched her hand a little tight. Released it.

'Louisa…'

'It's okay. Really. I've moved on.'

But had she? Regular people didn't panic when someone suggested a haircut. They just got a trim. They didn't get overwhelmed buying clothes, or in a bustling city. Did they?

'It's not okay. It will never be okay. For all my parents' faults, they were *desperate* for Felicity to be well. To imagine them actually making her sick… Why did she do it?'

That was the question that would never be answered. The answers died with her mother. All she could do was guess.

'I think it's because she was seen as a martyr, caring for my dad. When he died, she had nothing left.'

'She had *you*.'

The expression on his face was pained. Louisa gave a weak kind of smile.

'I wasn't enough. My mum and dad were everything to each other. Sometimes, for her at least, I think I got in the way.'

'I understand that sentiment.'

She looked at their hands, joined on the table. Giving each other support. They both had their crosses to bear.

'How was your mother found out?'

She withdrew her hand from his. Wrapped her arms round herself. Shrugged. 'I only know what I was told.

One time when I was really sick, a nurse became suspicious. Blood tests were off. My mum had contaminated my IV. People began watching then, put up CCTV in the room. It all unravelled.'

'There was no press. There was nothing.'

Louisa gave a short, sharp laugh. 'My mother was a Bainbridge. Of *course* there wasn't any press. The family tried to convince me not to say anything to the police. Said she wouldn't hurt me any more because she'd learned her lesson.'

Matteo sat across from her, his eyes darkening. A heavy frown on his brow. 'Is that when Mae took you?'

'Yes. And she promised me that everything would be okay. Nothing would ever hurt me again. That I'd always have food on the table, that I'd be safe. And she kept that promise, till the day she died.'

Matteo clenched his jaw so hard it was as if his teeth might crack. What that family had done. They would have returned her to a perpetrator so long as it didn't hurt the damned Bainbridge name.

Instead of her living the kind of life any child should have, there'd been attempts to silence her. Then she'd been taken in by Mae, who'd wrapped Louisa in a fantasy world. Didn't challenge her, didn't encourage her to live the life a young woman should. Instead, kept her in a kind of prison, one of safety and no risk.

Louisa needed more. She needed everything. A chance to explore the world and not be trapped by her own fears of it.

He was even more determined now to make the family suffer for what they'd done. To him, and to her.

'No one paid for what happened to you.'

'I'm free of it. That's enough.'

'Don't you want to be avenged?'

'I want to forget.'

Yet would she ever really be able to? That kind of thing left scars. She was still trapped by what had happened to her. He saw Easton Hall for what it was: a prison. He could show her a life that was something else. Something new to see every day. One on the move. He was an expert. In the meantime, if she wanted some forgetting, he could help with that too. He tamped his anger. Tried to remember that this night was all about her.

'We *were* here to celebrate you and your achievements.'

It was hard to tell under the magical string lights and in the candlelight, but he thought she might have blushed. She seemed to glow more rosily in the soft light.

'I guess we were, small though they are.'

'Don't undersell yourself. Your illustrations are magnificent.'

Now he was *sure* she blushed, her cheeks flushing a beautiful dusky shade. He didn't think it had anything to do with the cute pictures of frogs he'd seen. He bet it had everything to do with the other pictures. The erotic ones. Darker. No whimsy about them. All passion.

Then something changed in the mood of the evening. A switch, as if their sharing had opened a door of secrets, letting out deeper desires. He took another sip of champagne. Tried to shut the sensation down yet what he'd seen seemed to breach his barriers. She'd said she didn't want to get married. Her pictures were ones of passion.

What if intimacy was what she wanted, without messy and inconvenient emotion?

'Thank you. It's something I love, imagining that my drawings are bringing joy to children.'

She was lying to herself if that was what she thought they were talking about here. But he could see it. Children would adore her with her beautiful flowing dresses, her fiery copper hair. Looking like one of the magical creatures she'd drawn. They'd flock to her. He didn't know why that left a pang in his chest. A sense of... nostalgia almost. It made no sense, so he didn't dwell.

'Do you have any other projects?'

'Nothing immediate. I have some time to myself now.'

That was perfect. They were here, now, yet there was a whole world waiting out there for her. Properties everywhere. All the time he needed to show her what she was missing.

Course after course materialised. Magnificent dishes local to the area. More champagne, which she'd begun to savour. The little bubbles tingling her tongue, the sensation like happiness sparkling through her. Something between them had changed over the meal. They'd each given of themselves. Shared their pain.

'A burden shared is a burden halved.' That was what Mae used to say. Louisa had never believed it before. She'd carried her burdens close because the telling had been too painful, but now?

It was as if a veil had lifted. The night appeared somehow brighter, everything around her seemed to gleam.

She ate the last mouthful of a magnificent dessert. Pannacotta. It melted on her tongue and she moaned.

'I'm guessing you enjoyed that?' Matteo said, his voice a little deeper, in a way, somehow raw.

'The whole meal, everything. Tonight. Thank you.'

'It's what you deserve. Never doubt that.'

If only she could believe it. Sometimes, the demons still dwelled close. That was what her dreams were about, which was why she drew them. When viewed in the daytime they seemed to have less impact.

'I don't think I'd be able to fit in a dinner like that too often. I feel like I could almost roll all the way home.'

Home...it was the first time she'd really thought about any place other that Easton Hall in that way. But Matteo's Lake Como mansion wasn't hers. It was just a place to lay her head. Wasn't it?

'If you're done, we can go. Walk. As you said, it's not far.'

'I—I'd like that.'

She relished the idea, because she didn't really want the night to end. She had a fear that if it did, she'd lose something that she'd never get back.

Matteo stood and moved to her chair, helping her pull it out. A prickle of awareness shivered down her spine, pleasure at his closeness. She shut her eyes for a moment, simply absorbing the sensation.

'It's a date.'

It wasn't. She needed to remind herself, once again, that it was something people just said. A turn of phrase.

But a date was exactly what she wanted this to be. She wanted it all, whatever 'all' was. A yearning simply overtook her, for the things that a young woman who'd had a normal kind of life with a loving family might experience. She'd never grieved it before, but she did now. Because her life had been about survival, getting through each day without fear. It had never been about her other needs being met.

It was as if those locked-in emotions began spilling out around her. That was the problem with sharing them. It was hard to stuff those errant feelings back in when the sharing ended.

They left the restaurant after saying their goodbyes and she felt almost giddy. The sensation unfamiliar, till she realised that it was something like happiness. Or perhaps it was just the champagne. Whereas once, all she'd wanted to do was melt into the shadows like a little mouse, now she craved to skip down the streets in a way that would draw attention to herself. To laugh out loud and not care who was watching.

She didn't feel like a mouse now.

Night had settled solidly over the town. The streets still awash with people. Some local. Some tourists. Eating at cafés. Talking. There was music, a jaunty kind of folk tune. Singing in the distance. People coming alive as she felt. She and Matteo ambled in silence as she took in the wonder of it all. The cobbled streets, the stone buildings. Geraniums and petunias blooming in pots.

'This is a gorgeous place.'

'I'm glad you like it.'

'With your Italian heritage, will you keep looking for your birth parents?'

He shrugged. 'I'm unsure. I was trying to find out about myself, my history. The Bainbridges love their family stories. Mine. My *real* story, became…important somehow.'

The Bainbridge family had never been titled. Their

money derived from trade, a brickworks in the distant past, which meant, no matter how much money they held, they had always been seen as something less. Yet their once vast riches meant power, and that power opened doors. Tarnished now by poor management and a belief that things would always remain the same. Riches squandered.

But the power, it notionally remained.

It had never been used for anything good. And it hadn't saved her. The family name and preserving it was everything to the Bainbridges. Anything that might risk it was discarded, even people. Children, like her and Matty.

'Sometimes I think you can know too much.'

'I knew so little,' Matteo said. 'Apart from being dropped off at a hospital with a slip of paper pinned to my clothes, naming me Matteo. I suppose it was a kindness my adoptive parents kept my name. Or perhaps it meant they never really saw me as their family in the first place.'

'I'm sorry,' she said. They'd left the town centre now, moving towards the lake. 'But I think family's more than what you were born into. Anyhow, you can make your own.'

'I don't want a family. From past experience, they're vastly overrated. I prefer being on my own.'

She laughed, acknowledging the truth of that statement. 'Yeah. They are, aren't they?'

They began laughing together.

'We shouldn't, you know,' she said, through giggles. Wiping tears from her cheeks. 'It's not really something to laugh about.'

'Better that than cry, Lulu.'

He'd used her nickname. A warmth settled over her as she wiped the tears of mirth away, bittersweet though they were because they were born of a shared pain. An *understanding* settling between them.

'What if I'm crying from laughing?' she asked, and they both laughed some more.

When had life ever been so much fun? She'd enjoyed the days tourists came to Easton Hall. Dressing up like one of the past women of the house. Showing people round. Answering questions. But she could never remember a time where her life seemed suffused with simple happiness like this.

They began to walk down a slope. Her shoes slipped a little. Matteo steadied her. 'Take my hand. I don't want you to fall.'

She slid hers into his and Matteo simply *engulfed* her. His strength, his solidity. A breeze caught them as they strolled hand in hand along the roadway back to his villa. The air sweet with the drifting scent of citrus blossom. She looked up as they left the lights of the town, a few stars winking in the sky. The moon, bright and bold. Lighting their way.

It was perfect.

It's not a date.

Though what did it matter if she pretended, just for a little while? She'd never go on a real date, and imagining didn't hurt anybody. As always, her imagination had been the safest place for her to reside.

'On a moonlit night you get a beautiful view of the lake from a balcony upstairs. When we get back home, would you like to see it?'

He'd used the word home again. It struck her that it was the first time he'd said it in a way that didn't seem pejorative.

'I'd love to.'

The large iron gates of the villa loomed in the distance. They made their way to the house then he led her upstairs to a private balcony she'd not visited before. The lake lay ahead of them, an inky mark on the landscape. Along its edge, towns and little villages glittered. Lights weaving up the hillsides like threads of silver and gold stitched into the landscape. The moon rose high in the sky, painting a silver stripe on the rippling surface of the water.

She stood there, her hands on the balustrade. Giddy with it all.

'This is so beautiful.'

A breeze picked up; swirling round them. She clutched at her wrap and shivered. Not from the cold as such, but from…she didn't know. It overwhelmed her. The dinner, this. So perfect. So romantic.

The emotion of it all. The need pulsing through her with every heartbeat.

When had someone cared for her like this? As if she was a woman, and not something fragile and breakable. Broken.

'You cold?' Matteo asked, shrugging off his jacket. Draping it gently round her shoulders. 'Here.'

The residual warmth in the clothing left from his body seeped into her. The scent of him, rich spice, enveloping her. Going to her head. Matteo drew her close, then. Gently, almost reverently. Wrapped his arms loosely round her. She didn't know what to do with any of it, but the way he felt… Strong, solid. Louisa relaxed into his arms. Placed her head on his chest. Closed her eyes. Allowed herself to imagine that this meant more. That it could go further.

Allowed herself to simply *want*.

Heaven and hell were this, standing here in the silvery moonlight with Louisa, soft and pliant. Relaxing into his body. As she nestled into him, he was struck by a startling sensation. In his arms was where she was meant to be. He didn't want to let her go.

His body reacted in a way that he might have said was an inevitability, holding a beautiful woman. All the while a voice inside tried to tell him this was not right. He had a job to do here. She was work, another responsibility.

None of it mattered.

Everything about this was as right as a moment could be. Yet something niggled in the recesses of his brain. A warning that things were about to change.

What was life without change? As far as he was concerned, it remained the only constant. Anyhow, Louisa needed some care. Some kindness. He could never have imagined the deprivations she'd suffered. A little girl, losing her father. Hurt by her mother. Yet the family had tried to convince her to stay silent to preserve the Bainbridge name?

They were rotten to the core whilst pretending to be good. How many of them saw what was happening to her and simply ignored it? The volcanic sensation bubbled inside. Rage at the injustice of it all. The need to avenge what had happened to her rising up like magma inside of him. His arms tightened around her, drawing her even closer and then the heat turned into something else. A flame that simply flicked to life inside him like a pilot light. Desire for something else.

For *her*.

He couldn't unsee her fantasies inked into the pages of a book. Running like a film reel through his head. She was an adult with wants too and it seemed she'd been denying them for years. Living a solitary life in the country, hidden away. Jewels like her shouldn't be hidden. They should be brought out to sparkle. He could show her *everything*. Her hand lay on his chest, thumb gently stroking him. Did she even realise it? The way she was pressed into him, as if wanting to meld into his body? She might be an innocent, but she had desires. He wanted her. What did it matter if she wanted him too?

She shifted in his arms. He loosened his hold as she lifted her head from his chest. Louisa looked pale and ethereal in the moonlight. Wearing his jacket. Something primal and possessive gripped him.

'I can't thank you enough for tonight,' she murmured. Her voice somehow lower, huskier. The sound arrowing right through him. His arousal sharp, all-encompassing.

She shouldn't give him thanks. He was a bastard, both literally and figuratively. A cold, hard businessman who knew what he wanted and took it. People respected him and sometimes cursed him, but never gave him thanks. He found he wanted it, wanted hers, all for himself.

They were so close. The moment perfect and fragile, bathed by the magical moonlight, where it seemed any-thing could happen. Her hands smoothed over his chest. Almost as if she was trying him out. The slow slide over his pectorals and up to his shoulders where they rested.

He was hard. Aching. Matteo had sampled the earthly delights of any number of women and he knew the signs that someone wanted him. Yet part of him was all uncertainty, when uncertainty was something he didn't do. For some reason he knew that she had to take what she wanted from him. Make the first move. His instincts had served him too well to ignore that if he tried to push too hard the night would end.

He wanted this to be only the beginning.

Not of a relationship, but of an awakening for Louisa. If she could just open herself. To life…to him, she'd see what more she could have, and it would change her whole world.

'You deserve all things good, Lulu. Never doubt that. You've denied yourself enough.'

'You think?'

'I know.'

He gently circled his thumb on her lower spine, and she trembled in his arms, pressed herself against him once more. She'd feel what she did to him. There was no hiding it. She flexed her hips against him and if he hadn't already been standing in the moonlight under the night sky, he might have seen stars. Her little gasp, the soft intake of breath, was better than the music of an angelic chorus. He'd never experienced desire like it. Something lit inside him with a rush, like fuel to a bonfire.

'It's time to ask for what you want, then take it,' he said, his voice rough with need. Yet he knew the value of waiting. The benefit of gentle to break down walls rather than hitting everything head-on, with a sledgehammer. He was a patient man, and he could wait for her.

'Be brave, Lulu.'

* * *

Be brave...

She was in the arms of a man that she could no longer deny she was attracted to with a relentless craving. She'd pretended her interest was somehow detached, that he was a magnificent man but that it didn't really affect her, that what she saw in him was somehow removed from who she was. Somehow...academic.

All lies.

Louisa wanted him with a ferocity that should make her afraid. He wanted her too. There was no mistaking how she affected him and that gave her a surge of something that felt a lot like power, when her whole life she'd been powerless.

Not any more. This man did things to her. Lit a fuse that made her come alive in his arms. She wanted more of it, needed it like her next breath of air, like the food on her plate.

Ask for what you want, then take it.

Him.

How did she ask for that? This was all new to her. Old fears began to chatter away in her head. That she didn't know what she was doing. That she'd make a fool of herself. Louisa refused to listen to them, listening to her instinct instead.

She wanted to thank him, so she'd give him a kiss.

He towered above her and she felt so protected in his arms. Holding her as though he cradled something precious. Moving slightly, she stood up on her toes. Pressed her lips to his. Unlike the last time their lips touched he didn't move. His mouth soft against hers. She wasn't sure what else to do now, so she lingered for a few moments, hoping, before breaking away.

He'd done nothing, so that was that. Her great experiment. She could tick that off the list. Kissing Matteo twice. Brilliant.

Then he smiled. It was a slow metamorphosis into wickedness, the way his lips curled in that knowing way of his. He lowered his head to her as she tilted her head up. Hoping and praying that he was going to kiss her back. Instead, he moved his lips to her ear. Said nothing for a moment, seemed to simply breathe her in as if he wanted to absorb her. His breath caressing the side of her neck, making her tremble with desire.

'Do you want me to kiss you back?' he murmured.

She hadn't asked for what she wanted. Now he was forcing her to tell him. The whole of her was a pinpoint of yearning. Her breasts ached, nipples hard points in her bra. Needing his touch to soothe them. She'd thought she'd known emptiness, but she'd had no idea. This. Imagining him filling her. It was like an obsession, a drumbeat pounding inside.

She knew what would happen if she said yes, and she didn't care. It was time to be brave.

'Yes.'

He moved then. His nose gently drifting over the soft skin behind her ear. The sensation overwhelming her. She relaxed into his arms as he slid one hand onto her backside, drawing her close and flush against the hardness of him. Then his lips began to move, skimming over her neck. The tip of something slick and smooth drifting over her skin, then cool air. His tongue. As if he was tasting her.

Matteo gave...not a moan as such, but a pained exhale. It mirrored her own.

He lifted his lips from her body and looked down at her. His gaze almost assessing. She knew what this was, a pause to allow her to say stop. No. She didn't want him to stop. She wanted this moment to never end.

After a few heartbeats his assessment, or whatever it was, ended. He dropped his head and simply *claimed* her. She'd marvelled at how soft his lips were on such an uncompromising man, but there was nothing soft about the kiss as his mouth took hers. Her own began to move, like instinct. Wanting more, wanting everything. His tongue teased her lips and she opened to him, letting him in. An entrée to the main meal. Somehow, he managed to make the kiss so many things. Coaxing, encouraging, demanding. She simply fell into it. Let it overtake her. Rejoicing at his hardness against her softness.

Then the kiss slowed, but she chased more. What if that was all she got tonight? Her body was ready to fuse with him. To become part of him. It was as if she'd die if she didn't. Needing him to fill her.

He gave a wicked, low chuckle that rippled right through Louisa's body. It could have sounded mocking except for his arousal pressing, insistent, against her. She'd done that to him. Made this uncompromising man want *her*. Matteo traced a finger down the side of her face, her neck, the top of her chest, a light, feather-like stroke. Barely there yet it set her on fire. Her nipples burned as that finger made its way lower, towards the top of her breast and then...

It stopped. She whimpered. Wanton and needy.

'Am I neglecting you? Do you need something more?'

He leaned in, his lips close to her ear. 'Do you want me to stroke your nipples, ease their ache? Make you come?'

His breath feathered over her throat as he kissed there. A hand sliding up her waist to rest just under her left breast, waiting for permission.

'Yes. Please.'

His lips found hers again as his left arm drew her close once more and his right...it slid up, the lightest of brushes over her nipple, which beaded and tightened under his ministrations, heat spearing between her legs. Setting her on fire.

Could she come like this? In the dark of night when she allowed the fantasies from her drawings to overtake her, her own orgasms seemed to be hard-fought yet in some way feeble and lacking.

Now, she was overwhelmed by the sensation. The conflicting feeling of being so full yet so empty, all at the same time. He kept stroking her nipple, and she began to move against him, wanting and wanting...just *more*. It was like the most exquisite torture. She didn't know how she'd survive it. Didn't know if she even wanted to. Any desire for self-preservation simply fled under his talented hands and mouth. In this moment she would have done anything for him.

There was no slowing, he simply tore his lips from hers, breaths coming in heavy gusts. Her own lips well used, plump and tingling.

'I want you. I want everything.' He growled as if the words were wrenched from him, almost sounding inhuman with the need he clearly felt himself.

The power of that tore through her. That she could do this to a man who no doubt had vast experience. Who could likely have the pick of any woman he wanted, and still he wanted *her*. She stood at a crossroads. All her life had been about safety. Being a passenger. Now, she wanted to take control. To take something for herself.

Matteo. She wanted him. She'd had so little voice of her own, as a child. Trying to find it as a broken teenager. Yet even into adulthood she'd held something back. No longer.

'I want everything, too.'

'And what do you think "everything" is?'

He was making her say it, be explicit. So there'd be no misunderstanding. If she made this choice, it was because she'd voiced her desire openly, with clarity of mind.

She'd never wanted anything more.

'Sex. You.'

His exhale sounded part pained, part relieved. 'Take my hand.'

He held his out. Another choice between yes and no. There was only one answer tonight. Yes, always yes. She slipped her own hand into his without hesitation. Greedy for his touch. His grip as he curled his fingers round hers firm but gentle.

Matteo led her back the way they'd come. Through the doors from the balcony overlooking the lake, inside. Her legs barely carried her, weak with need. Time slowed, as if she moved through syrup. Such sweet anticipation with the spicy thrill of something else.

Desire.

Then Matteo stopped. Was he having second thoughts? Instead, he turned to her. 'This isn't fast enough.'

He swung her into his arms as if she weighed nothing. The sensation of being cradled, held in his strong arms, an overwhelming one. Like the night he carried her out of Easton Hall. Saving her. Yet this night, there was none of the fear. Only anticipation. In that moment as he strode through the villa, it was as if she was the most precious, cherished being on earth.

They crossed the threshold to a room she presumed was his bedroom, light to semi-darkness. Only illuminated by the moonlight through the windows and a glow from his en suite bathroom. He set her feet on the floor but he didn't let her go, as if knowing that she needed to be held, or she might sink into the carpet in a puddle of desire.

Whilst she could combust from the *wanting*, Louisa had to tell him. That no matter what those drawings might have implied, she was a virgin. Yet what if he hadn't realised, didn't want her?

Be brave.

'I've never done this before,' she whispered.

His arms tightened around her for a moment, as if to comfort.

'I know. Don't worry, I'll be careful.'

His words made her feel somehow...lacking. She wasn't some porcelain doll that could be broken easily. 'I—I don't want careful.'

She wanted...wild. Unfettered. Untamed. Something that took her out and away from herself. Made her feel like a woman.

'Then I'll take care. Do you want more lights on?'

She hadn't thought of that. She wanted to see him with his shirt off. His muscles, his own desire as he looked at her. But something else made her hesitate. Would he judge her, her body? No doubt he was experienced. Would he find her in some way lacking?

Her mind raced.

'I can hear you thinking, Lulu. So I'll take it the answer is negative. How about you relax and I make the decisions for a while? If there's anything you don't like, you can say no, and we stop.'

She nodded, her heart a pounding ache in her chest. Not of fear, but of anticipation. He took his jacket from her shoulders and tossed it onto a chair. Unhitched the chain belt from round her waist and dropped it to the floor. Grabbed the sides of her dress and pulled it, ever so slowly, over her head where it followed her belt. Then he unclipped her bra, eased the straps over her shoulders and cast it aside. She hesitated, wanting to raise her arms. Cover herself.

'No. Never hide your beauty. Stand proud. Let me look at you.'

She did. Arms by her side as he stood back and simply stared.

'You're magnificent,' he said, his voice rough with promise and desire. 'Lie on the bed.'

She did as he asked. Stepping out of her shoes and pulling back the soft covers. Climbing onto a bed that felt like lying on a cloud. But she didn't know how to lie there, in a way that seemed bold. On her back? On her side? Then Matteo pulled off his shirt and any logical thought fled.

The moonlight streaming through the windows illuminated his magnificent torso that looked as if it had been cut out of marble in the cool light. Almost like the statue of David, she'd drawn in her sketch book. Broad shoulders, generous muscles. So magnificent that if he had been a sculpture, the artist would have wept upon its completion. He was every midnight fantasy as he strode to his side of the bed and came to her.

'Your trousers?'

'They'll come off soon enough. For now, it's about you.'

He crawled over the bed like some stalking animal. Kneeled between her thighs. Dropped his head and feathered kisses over her stomach.

'Tonight, I'll kiss every freckle I can see.'

She trembled with need as his kisses drifted lower, till his lips were on her underwear. His breath hot. Breathing her in. He hooked his fingers into her panties. Drew them down her body as goosebumps peppered her skin. Every part of her over-sensitised, as if all of her shimmered with delight at his reverent touch.

'Open your legs.'

His voice was a command she obeyed immediately. Never a question she was going to do what he asked of her.

'I'm going to touch you.'

'Please.'

She'd die if he didn't. Her world became a pinpoint of desire. The agony at the juncture of her thighs she knew only he could ease. He stroked his fingers along her upper thighs, feather-light, and she arched her back. Trying to get closer to him.

'I won't leave you wanting any longer,' he said. Slipping two fingers to her clitoris where she craved him most. Stroking. Circling in a slow, steady rhythm.

'I wish you could see what I'm doing to you. How hot

you are. How wet. How desperately your body wants mine inside you.'

She moaned. This was beyond her experience. Alone, in her bedroom, imaging, drawing, had been nothing but two dimensions. This was *all* real. Her breaths coming sharp and fast as the exquisite pleasure of his fingers wound her tighter and higher. He was right. She wanted him inside her, desperate for him to fill the craving deep in her core.

'That's right, Lulu. Open your legs wider, sweetheart. Let me slide one finger inside. See how good it feels. Do you want that?'

Right now, she feared she'd give him everything if he asked it of her.

'Yes, yes. Please.' Her voice breathless, barely able to make the words.

His clever fingers left her clitoris and she moaned again.

'So needy for me,' he said, almost sounding reverent.

She arched her back again as one of his fingers toyed with her entrance. 'This is going to feel so good. I promise.'

He slid a finger deep inside her and moaned himself. 'So hot. My God. Lulu. Feel what you do to me.'

He took her free hand in his, pressed it to the crotch of his trousers. The thick, hard length there. She whimpered. The size of him. Her body flushed as if fevered. He flexed his hips into her hand.

'Soon. But I need to make sure you're ready.'

'I am. Please. Right now,' she chanted. The ecstasy held just out of reach, driving her on. It didn't matter how big he felt, all fear fled in the face of this need.

'You won't be ready till you're only capable of sobbing my name.'

It sounded like a promise wound in an erotic threat. Another flush of goosebumps shivered over her.

'Now, let's get started on that. Feel this?' He did something inside her, found a spot with one finger that tore through her like an electric shock. Unbidden, a wail of pleasure ripped from her.

He chuckled, low and dark like some evil genius. Which she was coming to believe him to be, the way he manipulated her body.

'Two fingers now. Would you like that, Lulu? More?'

'Yes,' she said on a sigh. Barely able to voice words now, meaning he was on his way to make good his promise that she'd only be able to say his name. He slid one finger out and then there was a little more pressure as he inserted another, in and out, in and out as if testing her body.

'I want you to be ready. I want this to be good for you.'

Every part of her trembled, balancing on a terrifying precipice. Her breaths coming in sharp gasps.

'You're so beautiful. So perfect like this. So soft. Almost there, almost ready. So close.'

Then he did something inside again. Curled his fingers. Found the spot. 'I'll keep giving you what you need. We have all night. I won't stop. I promise. Don't fight this. You're on the edge. I'll look after you. Just let yourself fall.'

Her body shook as she fought to do exactly what he asked of her. That edge was so close, yet just out of reach. The torture inside her relentless, his fingers not letting up on their sensual assault.

'Come for me, Lulu.'

Matteo dropped his head, his mouth to her clitoris, licking, sucking, and she was torn in two, sobbing. Tears streaming down her cheeks as she cried out his name over and over.

Matteo drew Louisa close, holding her in his arms as she wept, gasping his name. The desire, craving her, needing her, warring with his need to give her this time to absorb the pleasure that had overwhelmed her. A voice in the back of his head whispered that he should feel guilty for what he'd done. But how could he feel guilt when it was all about pleasure? Showing Lulu the things she'd missed in her life. Sharing this with her.

He stroked his hand over her, murmuring that she was beautiful and perfect, till her sobs stopped and she drew back, kissing him. Her mouth fervent on his own. Demanding, desperate. He returned the kiss, her lips luscious and soft. Her hands tugging at his trousers, sliding over his skin as she tried to get closer.

He pulled back. 'Do you want more?'

'I want it all.'

Her voice was still tremulous, breathy. Breaking with emotion. It should have screamed a warning but the only chant in his head was yes. *Yes.*

He stood, undid his trousers, slower than he wanted but this was for her, a show. Time for her to back away. Louisa watched him, her eyes widened, but now gleaming with desire in the soft light, as her gaze tracked over him. He felt it, her appreciation. Firm as the stroke of her fingers against his flesh. When had it ever meant so much?

Matteo dropped his trousers, his underwear. Kicked them aside and stood, naked. She gasped and he wasn't sure what her sharp intake of breath meant. Desire? Fear? He clenched his fists, flexed his fingers. Waiting a few seconds for her to say something again. Then she licked her lips and the simple move almost unstitched his tight control right in front of her. He wanted to pounce on her, devour her, rather than taking the tender care that she deserved. He moved to the bedside table, grabbed a condom. Tore the wrapper with haste but sheathed himself slowly as she watched him roll it down his length, her lips parted. Lying there on the covers, her skin pale. Her freckles in beautiful relief like a thousand stars sprinkled over her.

He crawled back onto the bed, stalking towards her. She gripped the covers as if they were the only thing stopping her from grabbing him. He hungered for her touch. Matteo lay beside her, stroked his hand between her breasts. 'I need to be inside you.'

'I need that too.'

Matteo kissed her, his lips gentle caresses over hers, till she deepened it. He let her lead for a while, before taking over. Wanting to show her more pleasure than she'd ever dreamed. To be the only man…

No. He was the *first* man.

This was her start, not her ending. He was only showing her what was there for her, how life could be for a woman like her out in the world. Yet why did something dark and possessive overtake him in that moment? A craving to lock her away, keep her to himself. Keep her safe.

He ignored it. This was all about her freedom, not an

imprisonment. He eased a hand between her legs and they opened for him once more. Checking to see she still remained wet, ready for him. Then he moved over her, notched himself at her entrance, looking into the green pools of her eyes.

'You're so beautiful. I want to make this good for you.'

He began to ease inside, watching her for any hint of pain. Her eyelids fluttered shut as he moved, rocking into her. Deeper and deeper with each gentle thrust into the tight, hot depths of her till he could go no further. He groaned on her corresponding sob. The glory of it, unlike anything he'd experienced, like his first time it seemed so new.

Then he began to move and for a moment she lay there, hands flexing over his back. Till she began to move with him, as if driven by instinct.

'Good?' he asked, the word grinding out of him.

'So good.'

They were the words he wanted to hear and he lost himself in the rhythm of their bodies. His mind blank to anything bar the biting pleasure. Her smooth skin. Her breathy sighs. His body wound itself tighter and higher as he thrust harder. Her movements becoming faster, un-coordinated. Her breathing more desperate as he drove her towards the edge again.

'Take your pleasure, Lulu. Take what's yours.'

She stiffened. Her fingers digging into his back as she pulsed round him on a wail. His mind blanked in a burst of white light and blistering pleasure as his or-gasm burned through him like an electric shock. Wip-ing him clean.

CHAPTER TEN

LOUISA HELD ON TO Matteo's hand as he helped her from the boat on his private dock. They'd spent the morning motoring about the lake. He'd taken her to see the village of Nesso, with its waterfall and Roman bridge. She'd watched as some tourists leaped into the lake for a perfect social-media moment, swimming and laughing. They'd explored Bellagio and strolled along the waterfront under sweetly flowering nerium, eating gelati in the sunshine.

How her life had changed since spending the night with Matteo. This need for him all-consuming. In the next few days after that first explosive evening, rather than exploring round the lake they'd spent their time exploring each other. Their bodies like undiscovered countries they needed to map with lips and hands.

She could never have imagined this life for herself, when the thought of even walking to the village round Easton Hall had filled her with a kind of foreboding. Something about telling Matteo about what had happened to her, that sharing, had released something inside her. How he'd pushed her just a little, had changed everything.

He'd talked about taking her to Paris, where something was happening with one of his hotels that might need his personal attention. Each day she found another place in the world he had a hotel or retreat, another place he'd explored.

He hadn't mentioned his quest to turn Easton Hall into another of his hotels. Perhaps he no longer saw the need? Life seemed so full and bursting with happiness.

'I have a challenge for you,' he said, pulling her from her thoughts.

'What sort of challenge?'

After settling her on the dock he smiled, and it made her warmer than the sunshine in which they stood. That smile of his could chase away all darkness.

'You'll see. I think you might like it.'

He took her hand again, so strong and secure. It was hard to know when she began to think of him like that. A place of safety rather than the man who wanted to take everything away from her. A pang almost like pain struck her belly. She wouldn't think about it. He hadn't mentioned anything. After what they'd spoken of, he must now understand why Easton Hall was so important to her. Anyhow, she'd overheard him talking on the phone to someone about repairs. Surely that meant they could return home soon?

As much as she loved the small slice she'd seen of Italy, Matteo's villa in Como, Louisa still yearned for that place to go back to. Cool and green. The place where her formative happy memories had been made.

'I can hear you thinking again,' Matteo said. 'Remember, you can always say no.'

That shook her from her introspection. The thing was, she didn't want to say no. Her life had been cloistered. Louisa realised how stuck she'd been and now she wanted to catch up. Experience what other girls at her school had talked about, before her imaginary illness had taken over her life. Travels with their families, dreams of kissing boys, adventures...she was making up for years of lost time. She said no so often, to invitations from people in the village, to the young man at the grocer's who'd asked her for a coffee once. She wanted her life to be full of yes.

'I trust you,' she said and squeezed his hand. He squeezed back. Instead of going to the house he led her through the gardens to an open-sided pavilion, surrounded by marble columns. Inside lay a gleaming blue swimming pool the colour of the sky, the water sparkling in the sunlight.

'I thought you might like to learn how to swim, or, at least, to get in the water and see what it's like.'

He'd kept his promise. When they'd first arrived here, she hadn't believed he would. But now...tears stung her eyes. He remembered. He hadn't forgotten.

Matteo let go of her hand and pulled his polo shirt over his head, tossing it onto a recliner that sat on the tiled surface surrounding the pool.

'Do you want to try?'

Her mouth dried. Would she ever get over the look of him? That caramel-brown skin, so different against her own. The hair smattering his chest, arrowing down to beneath the waistband of his shorts. Those muscles, ridged and rippling across his torso. She wanted to keep looking. She wanted to touch. Except...

'I don't have a swimming costume.'

'What a shame.' His grin in response was pure wickedness. 'Do you need one?'

She stilled, flooding with heat. The thought of him and her, bodies slick against one another. Then reality bit.

'People might see.'

'There's no one around. My staff have the afternoon off. If you don't want to, I'll just take a quick swim and we can do something else.'

He unbuckled his belt, undid his shorts and pushed them down. She'd almost hoped he'd be naked but he wore black swimming trunks underneath.

She nodded to him. 'That seems hardly fair.'

He laughed. 'Life's not fair, Lulu.'

He strolled to a panel on the wall and pushed a button. Louvres of the pavilion ceiling closed halfway. 'The sun's bright. I don't want you to burn.'

His thoughtfulness, it almost undid her. She could dissolve on the spot, right here. Matteo didn't seem to be aware of how he affected her. He turned and dived into the gleaming water. Swimming a lap of the pool under the surface before coming up at the other end then swimming back to her in freestyle, powerful strokes slicing through the water. When he reached the end he stood, water to his waist. Dripping from him like diamonds. Shook his head then ran his hands through his hair.

'Coming in?'

She looked out into the secluded garden. She caught a glimpse of the lake from here, but it was mainly hidden by shrubs. Nobody would see her other than him. Her heart thumped a skittish rhythm, something like nerves. He'd seen her naked before, and after the things they'd done she wasn't sure why nerves should hit her as if she were an innocent all over again. But she'd promised herself that she'd be open to these new experiences.

Her hair was in a long plait today, so she didn't have to worry about it getting knotted. There were really no excuses other than her own fears, so she took a deep breath, kicked off her shoes, grabbed her dress and pulled it over her head.

His wicked smile fell away. His mouth, partly open. A look crossed his face then, something far more intense and focussed. Desire written all over him. Her nipples beaded. All of her flushing under his admiring gaze.

'The stairs are right there.'

His voice ran rough across his skin as he pointed to the side of the pool. She unclipped her pretty lace bra. Wriggled out of her matching panties. Walked to the water's edge and put her toes in, the water cool against her overheated skin. Then she stepped ankle deep, down further to knee deep, then to mid-thigh.

Matteo held out both of his hands as she hesitated, trying to recall the few times she'd ever been in a pool before, experiencing the mix of joy at the feel of the water against her skin with the terror of what would happen if she went under.

'I won't let you go.'

'I know.'

She took both his hands as he walked backwards, and she stepped off. It wasn't deep here, yet her mother's voice kept whispering in her ear. *What if you drown?*

She tried to shut out the words. Matteo wouldn't let anything happen to her.

'What are you thinking?'

'How do you know I'm thinking anything at all?'

'You get a tiny frown, here.' He stroked a finger in the

middle of her forehead. A tiny drop of water fell on her face from his fingers. He gently swiped it away.

'My mother told me not to swim. She always asked what would happen if she wasn't there and I drowned.'

Matteo grunted. 'That woman shouldn't invade any of your thinking time. She never cared about what was best for you. I'm prepared to work diligently to make sure you forget what she's said to you.'

He drew her towards him, arms around her. His mouth descending on hers in a slow luxurious kiss she fell into, pressed against his body. The heat of him, the cool of the water. Delicious, conflicting sensations. Pressed together, she sensed him harden against her.

He pulled away, his breath coming hard and fast matching her own.

'I said I'd teach you to swim.'

'You did.'

'Let me take you deeper.'

She was already in way over her head. She tried not to think about what all of this meant. It probably meant nothing at all. She hadn't ever expected to have any kind of relationship. Love equalled loss, a dark and tangled web where those two things were inextricably entwined.

Though why she should be thinking about love right in this very moment, she wasn't sure. Love had no place here. He'd been clear he didn't want it, and neither did she. This, sex, it was enough.

He walked back and back, cradling her in his arms.

'Okay?'

She nodded.

'I did some research,' he said.

The idea that he'd investigated teaching her how

to swim, spending time she'd not known about, planning this for her, struck her as more than considerate. It showed that he cared. That he was beginning to understand what she needed.

'What did you find out?'

'That you need to learn how to float first. How about you lie on your back, and I'll support you?'

He helped her ease back in the water, his hands gentle against her body. Even though she knew he'd keep her safe, her breaths came a little too fast.

'I'll keep hold of you. Put your arms out. Try to relax,' he said and she did, looking up into slivers of blue sky through the louvres in the pavilion roof as she floated. The water caressing her naked skin as Matteo moved slowly about the shallow end. She shut her eyes for a moment, sound muffled by the water. Simply drifting on trust as he supported her.

'I'm going to let you go for a moment,' he said. 'I'll always be here, but you can do this on your own.'

His hands left her body for a few seconds, and she lay still in the water. No panic. No fear. Only trust that nothing would happen to her if Matteo was by her side. She didn't know how long she lay there, till his hands returned under her shoulders. Louisa opened her eyes, meeting with Matteo's own. He bent down, brushing his lips against hers.

'There was a terrible flaw in my plan,' he said. Shifting to lift her from the water up against him.

'What's that?'

'You're naked, and I want you.'

His arms snaked around her, pulling her flush against him. She wrapped her arms round his neck, her legs round his waist. He supported her as his lips met hers and they kissed. Deep and lush. She notched against his body, hard and ready. The friction delicious.

'I should be a better man,' he said as she tried to catch her breath.

'You are that man. I don't know why you don't realise it.'

He dropped his head to hers. 'There are things you shouldn't forget, Lulu. I didn't get to where I am without getting everything I wanted. Every time. Nothing stood in my way.'

But she was sure he hadn't found everything he wanted. He was looking for his birth family and hadn't found them. Had accepted he never would. She suspected he wanted a real family despite his denials. He didn't have that either. Matteo struck her as a man who was searching, and she wondered if he even realised what he was looking for.

'You can have what you want from me. I'm not standing in your way.'

His nostrils flared. Of course, she was talking about sex, but it was fun for a moment to be held here and believe that the possibilities were endless.

'Be careful what you offer me. You might find I take it, and I don't have much to offer you in return.'

She wished he could see just how much he had. How kind he'd been to her. And yet she didn't think he'd want to hear it, when it was clear there were things he couldn't accept about himself.

She flexed against him, and his eyes darkened to the richest of warm chocolates.

'You have exactly what I need right here, right now.'

He groaned and crashed his lips onto hers once more as she lost herself in the rhythm of his kiss.

CHAPTER ELEVEN

LOUISA SAT IN the warm morning sunshine on a sheltered patio overlooking the lake. She closed her eyes, relishing Matteo's gentle touch. The way his fingers threaded through her damp hair, separating the strands so they could dry.

'We should go inside soon; I don't want you to burn.'

'Just a little while longer,' she said, breathing in the scent of lavender that drifted on the breeze, which she'd always now remember as the smell of summer. Relaxing further as he stroked down her back. If she were a cat, she might start purring.

'It's like silk on fire,' he murmured as if to himself. 'Magnificent.'

'My family were hoping for the Bainbridge blonde.'

Matteo grunted. 'What have I told you about anything they had to say?'

Louisa opened her eyes. Stared out across the lake, like a well of blue ink on the landscape.

'To forget them. I do, mostly...'

Some days, the voice in her head could be persistent. Though around Matteo, the negative chatter had less power. His praise and his words tended to drown them out till they held no more irritation than a gnat she could swat away.

'*Mostly* should become *always*. They didn't deserve you.'

His grip on her hair gently tightened. Drawing her head back as she smiled. Goosebumps shimmered over her as his mouth descended on hers.

She opened for him. Their tongues touching, the kiss deepening. Each day seemed like a kind of miracle. A dream she didn't want to wake from. *This* was far better than any reality she'd ever lived in. And Louisa knew reality would have to intrude eventually, but she had time. There were no pressing deadlines. She could continue to drift in this warm, sunshine-filled fantasy for a while longer.

Matteo's phone vibrated on the table close by, drawing her from the moment. An interruption from the world that wasn't polite enough to stop for them. She drew away.

'Take it. I know you have a business to run. I'll be here when you get back.'

He smiled and it was warmer than any sunshine she might be sitting in. 'I'll hold you to that,' he said as he grabbed the phone and wandered into the house.

She stood and strolled to the railings of the patio overlooking Lake Como. Little boats skipping across its surface. Louisa had never thought she could love anywhere as much as Easton Hall and its surrounds, but this came close. In the UK, everything was about the safe and familiar. Here? She wondered whether she'd love it without Matteo. Because everything about the villa was bound up in him. This patio, where they had a breakfast under the dappled shade of enormous potted olive trees. Their days filled with exploration of the lake and its surrounds. Nights filled with exploration of each other. A sense of no end date. Just a future with a person not a place…

No, that couldn't be right. No futures had been discussed. Except he had offered to show her the world, his hotels, his retreats. His other houses. *That* was a future of sorts. And their nights, his whispered words in the darkness, of being unable to get enough. Of more, more, *more*. What was that, if not a future? Her heart fluttered against her ribs. Not a sensation of dread but one of excitement, of possibility.

The sun brightened, warmer as the morning aged. Matteo would worry if she burned, so she moved to a large cantilever umbrella he'd had set up here, so she could sit under cover whilst looking out over the lake. That care, that kindness. It meant something, didn't it?

Movement at the door drew her from her introspection. A liquid heat flooded her veins as Matteo stalked through. She couldn't get enough of him. His power. Strength. It all made her feel safe, protected. *Wanted*. She might *never* get enough of him. Except…

The look on his face. Jaw hard. Eyes narrow. His body not lax and loose but strung tense like a bow. Obviously, business was not going well.

'Problem?' she asked.

'The family seek to challenge the will.'

It was as if her heart forgot to beat. Like everything, the breeze, the birds, all…stopped.

'Can they do that?' She could barely get out the words. That they would try to take it all away…

'They've been rattling their sabres. Seems they're finally ready for war.' His fists clenched. Released. Looking as if he was priming for battle. He gave a short, sharp laugh. 'I expected it. They can try. But there's no doubt they'll fail.'

He strode to the balcony, planted his hands on the carved marble balustrade. Looking out over the lake, he reminded Louisa of a king, surveying his domain.

She stood, walked over to him. Her legs almost unable to support her weight. Her insides twisting in painful knots. What if they *were* successful? She'd lose her home. She'd lose everything.

This, here, Matteo's house on Como. She loved it, but it wasn't *home*. She'd be happy to travel, but there was a place of her own she always wanted to know she could come back to. Easton Hall. In that moment, she wanted to return. Ground her feet on the cool green grass, walk through the gardens, by the chalk stream with him. Make a home there, with Matteo. They could still travel together but they'd always have a place. It was then it hit her with a blinding strike of realisation, the endless possibility. How she…

How she *loved* him.

She could be his family. *They* could be a family.

'What if—?'

'No. This is the chance to truly destroy them.' He turned his head towards her, his eyes bright. Almost fevered with a zeal she'd never seen before. 'I own Easton Hall and they'll *never* get it. It *will* become part of my company's property portfolio. Generations will be able to enjoy it but none of them will be a Bainbridge ever again. It will be lost to the family for ever.'

Did he forget? He was a Bainbridge. Her mother had

been one too. And there was the not so small matter of her inheritance.

'But...what about me?'

'What about you?'

The words hit her like a slap. She almost reared back. He wasn't thinking of her at all. Hadn't she figured as part of his plan for a future, for anything?

'Easton Hall is my home.'

He snorted. 'You can live anywhere in the world. Pick a place. My hotels, my retreats, they're all available to you, free. Easton Hall is nothing but a crumbling symbol of a family that needs to be shown for what it is. Not paragons of virtue, but fake to the core. A façade for liars and cheats. You should have no interest in it, at all.'

'And yet, Easton Hall is *all* you can think about. You're obsessed with it.'

He wheeled round to stare down at her, nothing on his face other than the hard clutch of fury. 'Obsessed? I want to destroy what it represents. You should too after what was done to you.'

He still couldn't see. This between them was worth fighting for, revenge wasn't. It could only destroy, yet she finally saw a future and understood that love, the right *kind* of love, could build.

'Don't you see, Matteo? You say you don't care about place, don't care about a home, but you do.'

'You think you know me so well. You know nothing.'

She shook her head. He truly couldn't see, so blinded by hatred of a family that wasn't worthy of his time, it obliterated everything else.

'You said my mother shouldn't invade any of my

thinking time, yet you're not taking your own advice. Forget the family.'

'*Forget* them?' His eyes were wide, incredulous. A sneer of disbelief on his face. Yet he couldn't see what she could. Louisa needed to make him listen.

'Everything about you yearns to find *your* place. You've been searching for your birth parents. Discovered Italian heritage so bought a house here. What is all of that if not a need to find where you belong in the world?'

She hated the way her voice was so small, lost. Almost pleading. As though she had no agency here, when she did. She had the right to stay in the home till she decided to leave it permanently, or marry…

Marriage. She realised that with Matteo she wanted *everything*. Louisa reached out, settled her hand on his arm, the whole of him tense, as if one wrong move and he'd shatter. It was a surprise that he didn't pull away from her, but she had to make him see.

'You don't just want it. You *crave* it. Your safe place. Somewhere to call your own…'

Louisa took a deep breath to conquer her fear. To be brave and make her greatest pitch. To the man before her, to the boy he'd once been. To *Matty*. To the universe. To crack open her chest and hand him her heart. Hoping with every beat that he'd take what she was offering him.

Matteo pulled back, began to pace. How couldn't she see? This was his chance. The final hammer blow, and she thought he wouldn't take it? That some nebulous idea like 'home' could stop him? He'd never stop. Not until he got what he had planned for.

'I've told you. I don't *need* any of that.'

Louisa held out her hands, as if imploring him.

'You're lying to yourself. You own retreats. Boutique hotels. Escapes, sure. But they're still places where people live, for a while at least. Ask yourself why that's the business you chose. Why you're so successful. Your company is called Arcadia. I looked up what that means. A place of rustic idyll. Of innocence and pleasure. What does that tell you?'

He shook his head. She was looking for signs that didn't exist.

'It tells me nothing other than it's a lucrative business and I excel at it. My company's motto isn't "Beyond home, your ultimate haven" for nothing.'

She looked to the heavens, almost like asking for divine guidance. 'For a reason. Matty, can't you see? That just proves my point. You're searching and searching for your *place*, because you're lost. And now you're trying to take away the only home I want. Where I've always been safe. The home I believed I'd live in for the rest of my life.'

She didn't feel safe with him? Her words were like a knife to the gut. Louisa couldn't see. She was still trapped by her past.

'You're a young woman. You need—'

'I need to be where I'm happy. We both do, and I realise where that is. You don't have to search any more. I love you Matty. Make your home with *me*.'

Her words brought him to a halt. His heart pounding a sickening rhythm. No.

'You don't love me.' That was impossible. Matteo knew he should care but couldn't. Not with this sensation of heaviness in his chest. His heart pounding as if it would burst from his ribcage. She'd offered him something he didn't want. That he'd never asked for.

'You don't get to tell me how I feel,' she said. Something about Louisa seemed to crumple, fold in on itself. As if part of her had broken. She turned her back to him, voice cracking. 'And you don't get to tell me what I want out of my life...'

Matteo raked his hands through his hair as that heaviness increased. Squeezing the life out of him. There wasn't enough air to take a breath. 'I thought you'd be the one person who could understand. That family wanted to silence you. Send you back to the woman who hurt you to preserve their pristine name. The family who cast me aside because I wasn't a true Bainbridge, no matter what my adoption made me at law. They're craven and soulless, and they *will* pay.'

Victory was so close he could almost taste it.

She shook her head. 'How do you expect to make them?'

'They want a fight, they'll get it. There are reasons why Mae left the home to me. A right to reside to you. I believe those reasons have everything to do with the way that family treated us. It'll all come out in court, if not before...'

All the colour bled from her face, as if she'd seen a ghost. Her eyes widened.

'How could...how can...? You know what will happen. It'll be splashed all over the press.'

He laughed. That negative press would destroy the family and the image they'd built. The damage would be irreparable.

'It's perfect. They sow the seeds of their own demise. They won't even see it coming till I have them.'

'No!' She slashed her hand through the air, stalking towards him, fists clenched. 'I don't want that story to become who *I* am because that's all anyone will ever remember about me when they hear it. You want to use my pain, what I went through, as fodder to get back at the family I've left in the past. You care about revenge more than you care about me.'

He gritted his teeth. She thought to take it all away from him? What he'd worked at for so many years? For what, some meaningless declaration like *love*? His parents had told him they loved him, and they'd abandoned him when someone better came along. And where had love got her?

'If you cared about *me* at all, loved me as you claim, then you'd understand. But you *don't* love me. That's an illusion.'

Louisa's shoulders slumped. Her chin trembled as she took a shuddering breath. 'I—I thought…but I was wrong. I've told you before I'm not leaving Easton Hall. I thought you'd understood. I won't be a party to this, I can't stay and watch this happen… Because it will destroy everything.'

Louisa turned and began to walk into the house.

'Where do you think you're going?'

She didn't break her stride, kept moving as he followed. 'Away. Anywhere but near you.'

It was as if a weight pressed on him. Relentless. Crushing. Right now, he felt like Atlas, trying to hold up the sky. She wouldn't leave. She *couldn't*.

'You'll *never* survive on your own.'

Louisa stopped then. Turned, slow and deliberate. Head held high. Jaw clenched hard. Eyes narrow, spitting fire.

'Just you watch me.'

Matteo paced through his Como villa, to a window overlooking the lake. The day outside gleaming beautiful and bright. Blue skies and sunshine. A perfect day for exploring the small inlets, villages and surrounding countryside. Yet nothing about this was perfect. In a place he'd always felt settled, nothing seemed to fit any more. *He* didn't fit. It had been a week since Louisa had turned her back and walked away. In his arrogance, he'd been sure she'd return within an hour after she'd left. Then time had ticked by and night had fallen. There'd been no tearful return. Only silence.

A sensation had clawed at him. Fear. That she was alone and he wasn't protecting her as he'd promised. *Damned promises.* He'd gone to the village and searched. Silently stalking the streets and laneways. Visiting the *trattoria* they'd dined in, but she'd melted away. He might have called the police, had he not received a message via his assistant saying Louisa had been in touch to ask that he pack up her things and she'd provide a forwarding address.

That address hadn't yet come. Now thoughts of her plagued him. Was she safe? Did she have enough to eat? How would she cope without her familiar things? His gut wrenched at the worry that she was alone, together with a terrible sense that he'd forgotten something or, even worse, lost something irreplaceable. Because she hadn't walked away and left everything behind. She'd walked away and left *him*.

That distinction was vital.

He'd reflected on their final, terrible conversation. At first not understanding why she couldn't see that every living Bainbridge should be punished for what they'd done. To her, to him. That he had the means to lash out and destroy, as if that would somehow blunt the pain. However, he'd come to realise that the pain had turned inwards and now flayed him alive.

She'd offered him her love, and he'd thrown it back in her face. All because of fear.

Matteo turned away from the view that had once given him peace, and now reminded him of what he'd lost. He'd convinced himself that he didn't want relationships. Had spent most of his adult life alone, travelling, making his fortune. He still had everything he'd started this journey with, and had a fight ahead over Mae's will. As Louisa had requested, he'd asked staff to pack up her things, ready to send them to her whenever she gave word. They'd almost finished the job. There was one room left, which he'd told them to leave till the end. The room containing her drawing table and her art supplies...

He wasn't sure why he'd asked for that space to be packed up last. Hoping that she'd return, perhaps? But she wouldn't. Like his birth mother, like his adoptive parents. It was a familiar pattern. Everyone left him behind. That was why he kept moving. If you didn't stop, you couldn't be left. People had trouble *catching* you. Matteo started walking then. Not really knowing where he'd end up, yet at the same time finding himself unsurprised that he'd made his way to where Louisa had done her illustrations. After it had been so important to her, he'd found it hard to fathom her abandoning everything here. It told him how much she'd wanted to get away.

Her sketchbooks were stacked in a neat pile. He ran his fingers over the spiral bindings. The need to open them, to look, as if that would somehow connect him to her, became overwhelming. To immerse himself in the joy and innocence of her illustrations. Except he'd stolen that innocence from her. Tried to corrupt her. Taken a woman who deserved so much more than the cracked and broken man he was. Tried using her to satisfy his own needs.

He'd dismissed her as if she'd meant nothing to him at all. It was no wonder that she'd walked away without looking back.

He rubbed at the ache in his chest as he slid a random sketchbook from the pile. Flicked through book after book of whimsical drawings, sketches that he didn't understand. All the while the pictures connected him to her inner beauty. He marvelled at how untainted she'd been by what life had thrown at her. How she'd retained any sense of wonder at all was a miracle.

She was a miracle.

He took out the final book, one that looked a little different from the others. Opened the first page. Stilled.

An illustration of a little girl with flaming-red hair and a little boy, in a forest. A title page...

Matty and Lulu's Stupendous Adventures by Louisa Cameron.

It was as if his heart forgot to beat. Time simply stopped. He flicked through page after page. Stories of a sun-drenched summer where two sad and lost children found each other and made their own magic.

The memories of that time blazed on the pages. Funny, glorious. He'd forgotten how they'd found a nest of hedgehogs. Tried to catch fish with their hands in the stream. Sneaked through the secret passageways of Easton Hall, pretending to be chased by ghosts.

The only ghosts now were the ones he'd created for himself and they haunted him with a vengeance.

Back then he'd been a scared boy, full of bravado. He questioned how much had actually changed. The fear gripped him now, of what else he might find as he turned those pages. What other stories it would show. And yet there on the pages were tales of a holiday when two children were simply allowed to be themselves. A little boy, a little girl. Both of them perfect and innocent.

Somehow in the intervening years he'd lost that innocence, whilst Louisa had retained it. He'd spent his life building a business, accumulating money and for what? Because he realised it now. That childhood summer was one of the best times of his entire life.

No. There was something that eclipsed it. This present summer, before Lulu had gone.

How had he not recognised it? How everything had seemed softer focus, in so many ways, gentle. A glowing warmth that had nothing to do with the weather outside but was carried around inside him. An emotion so foreign he hadn't understood it.

Happiness, and something more.

Something expansive, that hinted at a future. Something vast, unfamiliar. Never-ending.

A choking sensation throttled him, an inability to

breathe. Lulu brought out something in him, a side that was patient, thoughtful. That could care and take care. Matteo gripped her art desk, riding the wave of panic and realisation. This emotion was all-encompassing. Something like he'd never experienced before, and that could only mean one thing.

He'd loved her yet had refused to believe it because everyone he'd loved had walked away. Like Louisa, except in truth that was a lie he'd told himself. He'd pushed her away. Ended it when she'd refused to be trapped in the same hatred and anger that had consumed so much of his life.

Hadn't he done the same to his sister as well?

He sat down with the book and finished reading the stories. Some he remembered. Like eating berries till their fingers were stained and bellies were full. Others he'd forgotten, like trying to talk to the bees after Mae told them she'd knocked on the hives in the days after Great-Uncle Gerald had died, letting them know that he'd gone but she would look after them. Whilst reading, he searched for a skerrick of that innocence inside himself. He wanted that again, the optimism. He craved it.

Almost as much as he craved a woman with flaming-red hair and a beautiful heart.

He slid his phone from his pocket. Thinking of the people he'd pushed away in the fear they would somehow leave him anyway. Losing them all the same because he hadn't had the courage or faith that he was enough to keep them close. That stopped now.

He looked at his sister's messages. Texts. The attempts to reach out that he'd tried to ignore. Took a deep breath. Called her number. She picked up immediately.

'Matty?'

'Flick. I'm sorry I haven't been in touch. It's been… busy. How are you?'

He tensed, waiting for the response. Was she well? Was she sick?

'I'm really well. Busy too! Hey…'

The conversation washed over him, about a trip she was taking to Australia nannying for her employer, as did the relief. One bridge being rebuilt. And he needed to learn how to do that properly before he attempted to mend what would be the most important, if that was possible. His biggest failing and greatest loss.

Lulu.

She'd offered herself. Opened her heart and made a place for him in it. For the first time in his life, he'd felt settled. Now it dawned on him that she was right. He'd been searching for a home. His surprise was finally acknowledging that he'd found it. Not in a place, but a person.

He needed her innocence. He needed her love.

He needed *her*.

And he would fight to get her back.

CHAPTER TWELVE

LOUISA SAT AT a small table on an ancient stone terrace overlooking Lake Como. The universe had put on another perfect sunny day for her, as it had every day for the two months since she'd walked out of Matteo's door. It hardly seemed fair when all she'd done for the first week was cry. Why couldn't there be rain, as if the world were crying with her? But she'd been delivered sunshine and, in the end, guessed it was said universe sending her a message. That no matter walking away from Matteo had felt like an evisceration, she'd survive it.

The world kept turning. Life went on.

After leaving Matteo she'd holed up in a *pensione* for a day, trying not to crack and break into a billion pieces. Not to drown in the tears that had fallen when he'd rejected everything she'd offered him. Her heart. Herself. Her love. Then she'd taken a deep breath and tried to make a decision. Her first instinct was to run back to the UK, back to Easton Hall. She'd called Mrs Fancutt, who'd told her the home itself was still under repair, but the gatehouse was empty. She'd considered it, but something about going back there felt like immersing herself in the past when, for now, she needed to start dreaming of a fresh future. Because who knew what would happen with the Bainbridge challenge to the will? She wasn't sure she could go back to Easton Hall only to have it taken away from her again.

Instead, here she sat, torturing herself in a tiny one-bedroom house she'd found on the lake for a good deal, when a long-term holiday letting had fallen through. She had money, she had time, and refused to allow memories of what had happened with Matteo taint this beautiful place. Of course, the universe had another trick up its sleeve. She looked across the wide blue expanse of water. A little boat zipping across the surface towards the small town in which she was staying. In the distance was a pale blotch on the landscape. In the days after she'd come to stay here, she'd discovered that what she could see across the lake was Villa Arcadia. Matteo's home.

'You'll never survive on your own.'

She rubbed at the ache in her chest. Those words cut deep. Of all the pain she'd suffered in her life, none had hurt as much as that. She'd thought Matteo had *seen* her. Come to know her. What a fool she'd been about it all, about him.

Louisa stood and left the terrace to stop herself gazing at a speck on the other side of the lake, obsessing over a man who didn't want her. She walked inside to where some sketchbooks and pencils she'd ordered online, sat on a rustic kitchen table. Here she was, surviving despite him.

She'd learned to cook with the help of the Internet and the generosity of the kind woman who owned the home. Who'd taken one look at a heartbroken English girl and had seemed to feel sorry for her, teaching Louisa how to make pasta. She'd found more work, another commission. Otherwise, Louisa tried to make sense of her life, to reorganise it, without relying on anyone.

The one good thing about what had happened was that she'd finally grown up. Her life wasn't in stasis as it had been when Matteo had first arrived on her doorstep, when she'd been frozen in time. Now she was growing into herself as a woman. If nothing else, she had that to thank him for.

Louisa slipped on her glasses, picked up a pen, and began doodling on the page. Scribbling little curlicues and circles, allowing her mind to wander. She'd been contracted to do some illustrations for a nature-themed diary. It was easy work. She didn't really have to imagine much. Only the changing seasons. Drawing animals, fruits and flowers. Yet her heart didn't seem quite in it. Part of that heart, she'd left behind in a villa next to a sun-drenched lake. Not her home, but the place she'd truly found herself.

She looked at the page and found herself drawing a little frog prince. Louisa dropped the pen, the ache in her chest intensifying. A sting in her eyes and burn in her nose. Despite saying it was something she'd never wanted because she didn't think she'd survive the inevitable loss and betrayal, she'd fallen in love all the same.

Yet here she was, alive and breathing. And even acknowledging the pain, she had to admit one blinding truth. Had she been given the chance to do it all over again she would, with no hesitation. Because those moments with Matteo were pure, unadulterated magic.

It had sneaked up and caught her by surprise under that warm Italian sunshine. All the laughter, and happiness and *wanting*. The sense that what was happening seemed timeless and endless. It was only at the very end that she'd realised what she'd been looking at was a future.

Then he'd taken it away from her, because he didn't want the same.

She wondered how he was. Whether he was fighting for Easton Hall and revenge against a family who had never truly accepted him. Whether he had found the peace and belonging that she knew he so desperately needed. But she couldn't worry about him. Revenge had no part in her life, letting the anger destroy her. Louisa knew there had been choices to make and, in the end, she'd chosen to save herself.

Which was what she was doing right now. She picked up her pen again. Turned to a fresh page, ignoring fallen frog princes. Was sketching out a few more ideas when a knock sounded at the door. Today was Wednesday. Working Wednesdays, she used to call them. Her life less rigid now, fewer fears about everything. She wondered who it could be. Perhaps the owner of the house. She'd promised to teach Louisa how to make gnocchi next, since Louisa had admitted she loved it so much. She left her chair and trundled down the stairs, opening the front door.

Against a backdrop of the glorious sunshine stood Matteo. In a polo shirt, wearing sunglasses. Hair, windswept. She gripped the door frame as her knees weakened. He was the last person she'd expected to see, and yet she drank him in like a woman dying of thirst. It didn't seem to matter what he'd said, the emotions came flooding back. The exhilaration, the despair. Jumbled together in such a potent mix and she didn't know whether to shout at him to leave, or fall to her knees and beg him to stay.

But his path didn't intersect with hers, so staying wasn't an option.

'Lulu.'

'Matteo.'

He winced, but he'd ceased to be Matty the day she'd walked out of the villa. When he showed her what he was prepared to do to exact revenge against a family who was not worth either of their time. Showed her exactly what he thought of her too. Rejecting her offer of love, of home.

'May I come in?'

She held out her hands. 'Can I stop you?'

He stood there looking as magnificent as ever. Tall, imposing. His skin a warm, tanned brown from days in the sun. Though now she noticed other things. He strangely held his shoes in his hands. His tan chinos rolled up to mid-calf, darkened with water at the bottom. They hung a little loosely against his lean hips. The stubble shading his jaw seeming to be more of a rough beard. How under his eyes had taken on as bruised an appearance as her own.

He looked like hell. It should have made her feel good, feel satisfied.

It didn't.

He gave a pained exhale. 'Lul—'

'No, just no. I'm not Lulu. You're not Matty. They were two children who should have grown up a long time ago. They don't exist any more.'

Why, after all he'd said, did she still want to reach out and comfort him? It made no sense, but she guessed love was like that. He was the man who'd shown her herself. Held up a mirror and forced her to look. In the process she'd liked who she saw, just as she believed he'd liked her too.

'I'll leave if you want me to.'

The thing was, she didn't. It made her angry. She was trying to get over him and he turned up here? How long would it take now to forget him after seeing him in the flesh? It was like some cruel game.

Still, she stood back, inviting him inside.

'Come on through,' she said. The space seeming to shrink with his imposing presence. He dropped his shoes inside the door then followed Louisa up the stairs to a tiny kitchen, where she put the kettle on. When the water boiled, she made a cup of tea for herself. He shook his head when she offered one to him, gripping the back of a kitchen chair till his fingertips blanched white.

'I thought you'd be living at Easton Hall.'

'It doesn't feel like mine now,' she said, leaning against the kitchen bench.

'You have a right to be there.'

'Do I? Really?' Louisa took a sip of the hot tea. 'I thought you'd be happy to find me here and not staking my claim.'

He rubbed his hand over his face. 'There are things I need to say.'

'I won't stop you. But I guess you should sit down rather than looming.'

She didn't want to be so sharp with him, but all those old hurts came flooding back. How she'd trusted him. How she'd believed in him. How she'd thought he believed in her too. And she realised in many ways that was her flaw. She'd been desperate to find things in others, things that she really hadn't developed herself. She'd expected so much of him when, in reality, he was only human. Just as she was.

He pulled out the chair. Sat. Seemed to try to make himself…smaller in some way. Perhaps he'd taken the looming comment to heart. She pulled out a chair and sat too.

'The family's claim on the estate…' he said.

She waited to hear whether they'd issued proceedings yet. Had resigned herself to the years of litigation. The crippling fear he'd reveal to the world what had happened to her, despite her wishes. No certainty over the outcome. No certainty about where she'd live. Because Matteo would tangle them up in litigation for as long as would cause the Bainbridge family the greatest pain. It was all so exhausting. So pointless.

'It's over, Lulu.'

Her heart rate spiked. She put her cup down on the table with a thud, although still holding on to it as if it were her only tether to reality. 'What do you mean, *over*?'

His golden gaze held hers. She was afraid of what he might see if he looked too hard. 'I needed you to know there's no risk to Easton Hall.'

Louisa tore off her reading glasses and tossed them on top of her sketchpad. 'What did you do?'

Matteo's gaze left hers for a moment, settling on the little frog prince she'd drawn. His focus seemed to be distant. The corners of his mouth kicking up before he came back to himself and turned to her once more, clasping his hands in front of him.

'Your home's safe. They won't be coming after it any more.'

Louisa sat there, mouth slightly open, hand clasping her cup of tea. She looked beautiful. With her hair wild and loose. Her verdant green eyes that had haunted so many of his thoughts, glimmering. It was clear she'd made changes in her life, moved on. Those changes appeared to have been good to her. When he'd spoken to Mrs Fancutt to check how the staff were faring back in the UK, she'd commented about it. Telling him he'd done well. That Mae would be happy.

Louisa's grown into herself.

Yet he'd done nothing except cause her pain. He wasn't responsible for her growth. It was all down to her. He realised she'd been underestimated. She'd kept her past with her mother so well hidden that no one recognised the depths of strength this woman held within herself, to merely survive.

Now, she was so cool and sharp. He deserved every part of her disdain. The hardness that seemed to coat her in a thin veneer. He hated that he might have done that to her. Might have made her somehow disappointed in life, because he was sure she was disappointed in him. That disappointment was the most painful wound she could have inflicted, because he'd realised in the days after she'd left that he'd basked in her approval like an elixir.

Craved it, because what he truly wanted was her love. A love she'd freely offered and that he'd unthinkingly rejected.

'How did you do it?'

'The why is probably more important.'

She narrowed her eyes. 'Yet that's not the question I asked.'

The burn was well deserved. She wanted answers, and he was here to give them to her. To apologise, to beg for forgiveness. To ask her to allow him to come back into her life. To say that he would take her love if she still offered it, and cherish her, rather than flinging her emotions back in her face.

'How did I get them to call off their legal action?' He shrugged. That had been the easy part in the end. 'I offered them money.'

A great deal of money, but he'd come to realise it didn't matter. Why should it, when his quest for revenge had lost him someone whose importance had become vital to him?

'That must have hurt,' she said.

The pain was nothing compared to the agony of watching her walk out of the door. Waiting for her to return in the assuredness she would, then realising she had no intention of coming back. Though he didn't think she'd want to hear that, not right now.

He shrugged. 'Money's nothing when compared to certainty. They did a lot of posturing, so I did a little of my own. I've been investigating their charities but haven't been able to pin anything on them. Just rumours, suspicions, reports that didn't add up. I warned them they'd attracted my attention and that they could use the funds to rectify what I suspected were anomalies in their accounts. It seemed they took my advice.'

Whilst he didn't have solid evidence, he'd seen the fear in their eyes. They wouldn't learn. One day they'd slip, and there would be no more of his money to bail them out. The regulators would catch them. He'd wasted too much of his life on them already, the hatred, the revenge. What he wanted to focus on now was love.

'Is that all you came to tell me?'

He had so much more to say. That life without her had become a cold, dark place. How, when she'd walked away, the meaning for everything he'd done in the past and what he'd worked towards in the future had simply evaporated. How he'd thought she was trapped in the past when the person who'd been trapped all along was him.

But even more, he wanted to reassure her that Easton Hall was safe. That she could live in it, and that he'd never try to take it away from her.

'I came to tell you that I'll continue with whatever repairs Easton Hall needs. Anything you want will be done. The house is your home to live in for as long as you want. For ever, if that's what you choose. Because all I want, Lulu, is for you to be happy.'

Louisa stood up, her chair scraping on the rustic tiles of the kitchen floor. She couldn't sit still. She wanted to pace. Only a few months ago this would have been everything she'd dreamed of. Yet she realised all of her dreams since leaving Matteo were still bound up in him. The passion, the pleasure.

That didn't make dreams reality.

'What if I don't want to live there?'

'Then you don't have to. After what you've inherited already from Mae's estate, you're a wealthy woman but, as you've reminded me, Easton Hall has been *your* home and you still deserve part of it. If you want to move away for ever, we can calculate the value of your right to re-side, and I'll pay you for it. Then you can go anywhere you want in the world.'

What did she really want? She wrapped her arms around herself, turned away and looked out of a small kitchen window to Lake Como and the tiny dot on the other side that was Villa Arcadia.

There was so much she had to say, she hardly knew where to start. Though, where better than one of the things that had hurt her the most?

'You said I wouldn't survive on my own.'

She heard Matteo's chair move out from the table. A prickle at the back of her neck. A slide of warmth tell-ing her he was close.

'I was wrong. You didn't just survive, you thrived.'

Thriving might have been a bit of an overstatement.

'How do you even know?' she asked.

He gave a short, sharp laugh. 'Don't you think in the days after you left, that I didn't look for you? I needed to make sure you were okay. I knew you'd left a *pensione* in the next village. Then I spoke to Mrs Fancutt and she told me you were still in Italy. In the end, I found you here.'

Her heart began to beat a quick and thready rhythm. She'd thought that he didn't care at all, that he'd com-pletely washed his hands of her, and yet here he was ad-mitting that he'd known what she was doing all along. That she was just across the lake from him. Then why did it still seem like an unbreachable gulf?

Louisa wheeled round, the burn of tears threatening. Her voice catching in her throat. 'You hurt me, Matteo.

You made me feel special and then you took that all away because revenge against the family was more important than anything. It would *never* be me.'

He took a step forward. Stopped. A moment of hesitation as if he was unsure of himself.

'I've never dwelled on my mistakes. I've lived a life with no regrets, believing that I was relentlessly moving forward. But, Lulu, I have regretted every moment of that last conversation with you. Analysed every word that would have caused you pain. I've obsessed. Immersed in a past I can't take back but wish I could change. I came to realise that anything I wanted, revenge, business, success, money, it was all hollow without you in my life.'

Everything stilled. It was as if she forgot to breathe, as if her heart had missed a beat. 'What are you saying?'

'I can't change the past, that's what shaped me. It's the future I have some control over, and I've come to realise that my past has held me hostage for long enough. I said I'd accepted that I'd never find my birth family, but I lied. To myself more than anyone else. You were right. I was searching and searching for something that never really existed. Now I've stopped.'

'I don't understand.'

'My whole life has been about temporary. I didn't believe another person could give me love. I figured deep down that you'd walk away and leave me, so I pushed you away as if that would protect me. Instead, I came to realise whether I pushed you away or whether you walked away on your own, that knife plunging into my heart hurt just the same. My search was for family when what I'd been looking for was standing right in front of me, imploring me to choose her. When I realised that, everything became easy. I want you. I choose you. I love you.'

Her back pressed into the kitchen benchtop, hands gripping the edges to hold her up, because she could hardly believe what he was telling her. 'You love me?'

'How could I not?' He began to move forwards again. 'You said I was looking for a home. When you walked away, I realised what I hadn't before. That home isn't a place.'

He was talking about a *home* now? What about the man who travelled the world, who never stood still…?

'You want to make Easton Hall your home, with me?'

He was so close. She tilted her head back to look up at him and the hard man of that last, awful day had simply disappeared. Melted away. All she saw was softness, for her.

She saw *Matty* again.

'Did you miss the part about me saying I love you?'

She gave a tremulous laugh. Was this a dream? Could this be real? 'No, I kind of got that bit.'

'*You're* my home, Lulu. Wherever you want to be, I'll be too. My place is with you. What I'd really like is for you to say you still love me too. But if you don't, if you don't trust me yet, then I'm prepared to work at it. Diligently.'

Everything seemed so shaky in this moment and yet heat began to flood over her. 'I really like it when you're diligent.'

The corner of his mouth kicked up in a wry grin. 'I hoped you might.'

'What if I said that I've never really loved anybody before? It feels thrilling, it feels terrifying, and I really don't have a single clue what I'm doing.'

He laughed. Rubbed a hand over his face. 'Don't worry, neither do I. We can practise together, till we make it perfect. But right now, I'd really like to hold you.'

Matty opened his arms and she walked right into them. He wrapped her tight. That comforting sense of belonging returned. As she relaxed into his embrace, his damp chinos brushed against her legs. She pulled back to look at him.

'Why are your trousers wet?'

The corner of his mouth kicked up. 'I motored across the lake to see you. There was no mooring, so I had to wade to shore.'

The little boat she'd seen, that was him. If she could have fallen even more in love with him in this moment, she would have. But that was impossible. Her heart was too full already. All the times she'd gazed out at his villa, just a speck in the distance. Wondering whether he was still there. What he was doing... 'Did you look across the lake to me?'

'Every day and every night from the time I discovered where you were.'

They'd been watching each other. Tears pricked her eyes and one escaped, tracking down her cheek. Matty gently brushed it away with his thumb.

'Marry me, Lulu? I can't bear the idea of another day away from you. I want to prove that we should never be apart again. We can forget everyone else and make our own family together.'

'You don't need to prove anything to me, Matty. I'll marry you because I love you. I can't think of a better reason.'

He threaded his fingers through her hair, brushed his lips gently across her mouth.

'There's no better reason in the world.'

EPILOGUE

MATTY TOOK LULU'S hand as they walked through the cool, soft sand on his Whitsunday Island resort, which he'd closed to other guests for the duration of their stay. A warm breeze blew, sunset painting the sky in pink and gold. It had been two years since their wedding, and for their second anniversary he'd decided to celebrate by re-visiting their honeymoon destination, where he'd shown her the beach for the first time.

'Where are we going?' she asked. Lulu looked beautiful tonight in a sheer and shimmery kaftan that moulded to every curve, the same colours as the sunset. Her copper hair loose, streaming down her back. Lit up like fire in the golden light.

He smiled. 'I have a surprise for you.'

She smiled back. He'd never thought Lulu could look more beautiful than she had on their wedding day, in a magnificent vintage wedding gown under a bower of roses at their Lake Como villa, but he'd been wrong. Each day surpassed the rest, as if she were created anew each morning, just for him.

'I don't need surprises. You're enough.'

She gazed up at him, her tropical green eyes filled with warmth and love. He understood, she was enough for him as well. He wanted for nothing with Lulu in his life. Each day, now complete.

Since their wedding, they'd spent time travelling the world, chasing summer. Visiting his houses, his hotels, and resorts. Even though they had plenty of places to stay they kept two homes. Easton Hall, now renovated to its former glory, and Villa Arcadia. Both, places of rustic idyll. Innocence and pleasure.

He looked down at Lulu, her gaze heated. Lips parted; pupils blown wide. A delicate flush on her cheeks. Okay. He grinned. Perhaps more pleasure than innocence… But he wasn't complaining. Life was an adventure in hedonism with his incredible wife.

An adventure in other ways too. After some thought and a little encouragement from him, she'd submitted her stories and illustrations about their stupendous childhood adventures to a publisher. Soon, Lulu would have a series of children's books in her name and could add author to illustrator on her résumé. Warmth like the sun kindled in his chest, his pride at her achievements. She amazed him every day, the way she overcame and grew. He gently squeezed her hand, she squeezed back.

'What are you thinking?' she asked.

That he couldn't wait to get to where they were going. Even though she said she didn't need it, Matty loved to surprise her as a way of thanks. For freeing him from the exhausting quest for belonging he hadn't even realised he'd been on.

'That every day with you is the happiest day of my life.'

She sighed. 'When I thought you couldn't make me swoon even harder… Oh… Matty… This is *beautiful*.'

They'd arrived at what he'd organised, a tent of jewel-coloured silk high on the beach. Surrounded by flaming torches, waiting for night to fall. The floor was covered with soft blankets, strewn with plush pillows. With champagne on ice and a basket full of delicacies, he had everything he needed to celebrate how much he loved her.

'You did this for me?' Her voice trembled, cracked.

'A romantic picnic for two,' he said. 'I've given the staff the night off.'

They wouldn't be disturbed unless he called for something. They were as alone as they could possibly be. Shipwrecked together. He led her inside, and they sank into the cushions. The waves a gentle hiss on the sand in front of them. He grabbed the champagne from the ice bucket, poured two glasses.

'A toast.' He held up his glass to her. 'Happy anniversary, Mrs Bainbridge.'

'Happy anniversary to you, Mr Bainbridge,' Lulu replied.

That once disparaged family name held no power over him any more. Not now that he and Lulu shared it with each other. It was only a name, not something that defined him. Anyhow, it was the name his sister carried too, and he loved her. With so much love in his life, there was simply no room for negativity.

Lulu looked out over the ocean. Blue turning to purple as the colours in the sky deepened. She took a sip of her champagne, put down her glass. 'It's going to be hard to leave here.'

'Where would you like to go next?'

She looked up at him and smiled. 'So long as I'm with you, the "where" doesn't matter.'

His heart felt as if it would burst. Matty put down his glass to join Lulu's as he leaned into her, cupping her cheek. Stroking his thumb over her soft skin. Their lips touching, their breaths mingling as the kiss deepened. Lulu slid her hand under his shirt, stroking his back as he became fire, each nerve setting alight as he eased her onto cushions behind them.

'Are you thinking of skipping dinner and going straight for dessert?' he asked.

Her breaths came in heavy gusts. 'I thought that was your idea.'

'Then dinner can wait a little while.'

'I was thinking…' Lulu's copper hair fanned out behind her. She took her lower lip in her teeth, worrying it. When she released it, he kissed the reddened flesh better.

'Yes?' he murmured against her mouth, contemplating where to kiss next.

'Maybe we could try for a baby.'

Matty stilled, sat up. They'd talked of family. Wanted children. But they'd never talked about a timeframe.

'Now?' he asked.

A baby. A family.

'It's what I was hoping, if you want.'

'I want *everything*,' he said, his voice rough with emotion. He stroked his hands over the silk of her dress, her nipples tight under the fine fabric.

'Are you…wearing anything under that?'

Lulu's lips curved into a seductive smile and his desire speared low and hard.

'No.'

He eased the filmy fabric over her head. Tossed it aside. She lay on the pillows and blankets beautifully naked, arms above her head. The sunset painting her skin rose gold.

His mouth watered. He was starving, but not for food.

'I see you came prepared.'

She laughed, the sound lighting him up like the flaming torches surrounding them. His breath caught as she tugged the hem of his shirt, pulling it over his head. She cast it aside as he worked his way out of his shorts and underwear till he lay gloriously naked as well, the sea breeze cool on his overheated skin.

It was as if they were the only two people left on earth.

'I need you,' he murmured.

'I need you too.' Her voice was a fervent whisper in the approaching twilight. 'Now. Don't wait.'

She didn't need to ask. He kissed her again. Moved over her body, skin to skin. Into her as she opened for him. Sliding deep, welcomed by the hot velvet depths of her as she arched into him with a moan. Losing himself utterly as they moved together in perfect synchronicity. Breathing each other's breaths, their hearts beating like one.

He'd never felt so unprotected as he lost himself to the ecstasy that was his wife. With thrusts and gasps and scorching pleasure they came as one. Shuddering. Replete. Matty was overcome by the same sensation as he'd experienced on his wedding day.

That this was the first day of the rest of their lives.

As they drifted back into reality, still joined, he looked down at her, Lulu's eyes dreamy and half focussed. A flush across her chest and throat. Lips plush, pink and well kissed.

'Every day, Lulu, you honour me,' he said. 'You are my beating heart.'

'I love you, Matty. You always hold mine.'

Whatever adventures were yet to come, they were in it together. For ever. Lulu lifted her hand, threaded her fingers into his hair. Pulled his head down.

'You showed me the world,' she whispered against his lips.

'You led me home,' he said before deepening their kiss.

And there was nowhere else in the world he'd rather be, than home with her.

* * * * *

HARLEQUIN
Reader Service

Enjoyed your book?

Try the perfect subscription for Romance readers and get more great books like this delivered right to your door.

See why over 10+ million readers have tried Harlequin Reader Service.

Start with a Free Welcome Collection with free books and a gift—valued over $20.

Choose any series in print or ebook.
See website for details and order today:

TryReaderService.com/subscriptions

RSBPA24R